GOLDEN HELL

SELECTED FICTION WORKS BY L. RON HUBBARD

FANTASY

The Case of the Friendly Corpse

Death's Deputy

Fear

The Ghoul

The Indigestible Triton

Slaves of Sleep & The Masters of Sleep

Typewriter in the Sky

The Ultimate Adventure

SCIENCE FICTION

Battlefield Earth

The Conquest of Space

The End Is Not Yet

Final Blackout

The Kilkenny Cats

The Kingslayer

The Mission Earth Dekalogy*

Ole Doc Methuselah

To the Stars

ADVENTURE

The Hell Job series

WESTERN

Buckskin Brigades

Empty Saddles

Guns of Mark Jardine

Hot Lead Payoff

A full list of L. Ron Hubbard's novellas and short stories is provided at the back.

*Dekalogy—a group of ten volumes

L. RON HUBBARD

GOLDEN HELL

GALAXY PRESS

Published by
Galaxy Press, LLC
7051 Hollywood Boulevard, Suite 200
Hollywood, CA 90028

Printed in the United States of America.

ISBN-10 1-59212-273-6
ISBN-13 978-1-59212-273-8

Library of Congress Control Number: 2007903542

CONTENTS

FOREWORD

STORIES FROM PULP FICTION'S GOLDEN AGE

AND it *was* a golden age.

The 1930s and 1940s were a vibrant, seminal time for a gigantic audience of eager readers, probably the largest per capita audience of readers in American history. The magazine racks were chock-full of publications with ragged trims, garish cover art, cheap brown pulp paper, low cover prices—and the most excitement you could hold in your hands.

"Pulp" magazines, named for their rough-cut, pulpwood paper, were a vehicle for more amazing tales than Scheherazade could have told in a million and one nights. Set apart from higher-class "slick" magazines, printed on fancy glossy paper with quality artwork and superior production values, the pulps were for the "rest of us," adventure story after adventure story for people who liked to *read.* Pulp fiction authors were no-holds-barred entertainers—real storytellers. They were more interested in a thrilling plot twist, a horrific villain or a white-knuckle adventure than they were in lavish prose or convoluted metaphors.

The sheer volume of tales released during this wondrous golden age remains unmatched in any other period of literary history—hundreds of thousands of published stories in over nine hundred different magazines. Some titles lasted only an issue or two; many magazines succumbed to paper shortages during World War II, while others endured for decades yet. Pulp fiction remains as a treasure trove of stories you can read, stories you can love, stories you can remember. The stories were driven by plot and character, with grand heroes, terrible villains, beautiful damsels (often in distress), diabolical plots, amazing places, breathless romances. The readers wanted to be taken beyond the mundane, to live adventures far removed from their ordinary lives—and the pulps rarely failed to deliver.

In that regard, pulp fiction stands in the tradition of all memorable literature. For as history has shown, good stories are much more than fancy prose. William Shakespeare, Charles Dickens, Jules Verne, Alexandre Dumas—many of the greatest literary figures wrote their fiction for the readers, not simply literary colleagues and academic admirers. And writers for pulp magazines were no exception. These publications reached an audience that dwarfed the circulations of today's short story magazines. Issues of the pulps were scooped up and read by over thirty million avid readers each month.

Because pulp fiction writers were often paid no more than a cent a word, they had to become prolific or starve. They also had to write aggressively. As Richard Kyle, publisher and editor of *Argosy,* the first and most long-lived of the pulps, so pointedly explained: "The pulp magazine writers, the best of them, worked for markets that did not write for critics or attempt to satisfy timid advertisers. Not having to answer to anyone other than their readers, they wrote about human beings on the edges of the unknown, in those new lands the future would explore. They wrote for what we would become, not for what we had already been."

Some of the more lasting names that graced the pulps include H. P. Lovecraft, Edgar Rice Burroughs, Robert E. Howard, Max Brand, Louis L'Amour, Elmore Leonard, Dashiell Hammett, Raymond Chandler, Erle Stanley Gardner, John D. MacDonald, Ray Bradbury, Isaac Asimov, Robert Heinlein—and, of course, L. Ron Hubbard.

In a word, he was among the most prolific and popular writers of the era. He was also the most enduring—hence this series—and certainly among the most legendary. It all began only months after he first tried his hand at fiction, with L. Ron Hubbard tales appearing in *Thrilling Adventures, Argosy, Five-Novels Monthly, Detective Fiction Weekly, Top-Notch, Texas Ranger, War Birds, Western Stories,* even *Romantic Range.* He could write on any subject, in any genre, from jungle explorers to deep-sea divers, from G-men and gangsters, cowboys and flying aces to mountain climbers, hard-boiled detectives and spies. But he really began to shine when he turned his talent to science fiction and fantasy of which he authored nearly fifty novels or novelettes to forever change the shape of those genres.

Following in the tradition of such famed authors as Herman Melville, Mark Twain, Jack London and Ernest Hemingway, Ron Hubbard actually lived adventures that his own characters would have admired—as an ethnologist among primitive tribes, as prospector and engineer in hostile climes, as a captain of vessels on four oceans. He even wrote a series of articles for *Argosy,* called "Hell Job," in which he lived and told of the most dangerous professions a man could put his hand to.

Finally, and just for good measure, he was also an accomplished photographer, artist, filmmaker, musician and educator. But he was first and foremost a *writer,* and that's the L. Ron Hubbard we come to know through the pages of this volume.

This library of Stories from the Golden Age presents the best of L. Ron Hubbard's fiction from the heyday of storytelling, the Golden Age of the pulp magazines. In these eighty volumes, readers are treated to a full banquet of 153 stories, a kaleidoscope of tales representing every imaginable genre: science fiction, fantasy, western, mystery, thriller, horror, even romance—action of all kinds and in all places.

Because the pulps themselves were printed on such inexpensive paper with high acid content, issues were not meant to endure. As the years go by, the original issues of every pulp from *Argosy* through *Zeppelin Stories* continue crumbling into brittle, brown dust. This library preserves the L. Ron Hubbard tales from that era, presented with a distinctive look that brings back the nostalgic flavor of those times.

L. Ron Hubbard's Stories from the Golden Age has something for every taste, every reader. These tales will return you to a time when fiction was good clean entertainment and the most fun a kid could have on a rainy afternoon or the best thing an adult could enjoy after a long day at work.

Pick up a volume, and remember what reading is supposed to be all about. Remember curling up with a *great story.*

—Kevin J. Anderson

KEVIN J. ANDERSON *is the author of more than ninety critically acclaimed works of speculative fiction, including The Saga of Seven Suns, the continuation of the Dune Chronicles with Brian Herbert, and his* New York Times *bestselling novelization of L. Ron Hubbard's* Ai! Pedrito!

GOLDEN HELL

CHAPTER ONE

ONE night in the Hotel du Pekin, a man uttered a statement which was to sentence me to more hardship and privation than I had ever before known, and to more danger, and to more high adventure than I had thought possible in this commonplace world.

Leaning on the bar and looking at me bleary-eyed, Charlie Martin said, "*All* Mongolians are rich."

Not much, but enough. Why were they rich? Certainly it wasn't commerce and it wasn't agriculture. That nomadic people, now that I came to think of it, had no visible means of support and yet—THEY WERE ALL RICH.

I am not what you'd call a romantic adventurer, neither an adventurer nor romantic. I don't happen to like the sound of either. What I've done has come under the head of experience and perhaps exploit and sometimes conquest. You might even call me hardheaded, determined to get what I want where I want it—and that, to my everlasting sorrow, is not a fitting or a fit code for any man.

I know all these things now and I didn't then. I know entirely too much how wrong I was. I've seen things since that night in the Hotel du Pekin which even now I can't believe I have seen. But the mental scars are there.

I am not what you'd call a romantic adventurer,
neither an adventurer nor romantic.

Had you asked me, there at the bar, "Do you believe in God?" I would have replied, "Well, yes and no," and in a bigoted way I would have explained a very complex conception to you. Now, to the same question, I would say, "I don't know. I've never had any great proof of God. But I know there's a hell. LOST UP THERE IN THE GOBI, I FOUND IT!"

In a careless way, you've heard men say, "I went to hell and back to get that." They didn't mean hell, really.

But I do.

This gold beside me, that diamond in this ring. I went to hell and brought them back.

Up there, lost in the Gobi, there's a mountain with a name so sacred to Mongols that even here I dare not write it. Why? Because that mountain has a festering wound in the craggy side, and through that wound, men pass on their journey to hell.

Charlie Martin knew a lot about such things. He was an archaeologist attached to a museum and he looked at all things in a sober, academic light. He went on to expound his theory of why Mongolians were all rich and it was too common for repetition.

As I parted with him that night, my mind was already dwelling on a wild idea which had come to me. I said, in a careless sort of way, "I think I'll take a run up to Kalgan and maybe beyond in a few days."

"Country's pretty wild right now," said Charlie. "Watch yourself."

I would have done very well to have heeded his advice, but I didn't. I was too immersed in this idea of mine.

All Mongolians were rich and they didn't have mines. But

the Gobi was a big place and who knew what you could find in those flat-topped scarps which rose like a child's blocks out of the gravelly waste.

Two days later I was on my way. Thanks to Charlie, I had a letter to the Prince of East Sung, a man very influential in the country, and I anticipated no difficulties.

You see, simple fool that I am, I thought that there would be gold up there, and if there was, what would hinder my scouting around, finding it and staking out a claim? I had a small gasoline-driven, dry panner with which to test those gravelly washes where no water ever flowed.

Gold is a driving force. It had taken me on a wild trek through the country of the ancient Mayas until the Yucatán Indians had driven me out. It had taken me through the upper forgotten mountains of Ecuador, and through the endless wilderness of northern Canada. I knew gold, but little else. I had a degree in mining, but the soberer jobs left me cold. I always managed to make my stake and keep going, nothing terribly rich, but enough. A mining engineer, when he takes the prospector's trail, doesn't experience very much difficulty. He can pass the old sourdoughs with their odd ideas and he can guess at things the so-called practical miner never suspects exist.

Young and confident, full of plans and enthusiasm, I arrived at the palace of the Prince of East Sung. The place was imposing, as yellow as the great plains and the Golden Mountains, built like a fort, ancient beyond the count of years. You had the impression of frowning dignity.

At the gate I was met by a cavalry officer, a fellow who bulked in his bursting furs like some overstuffed sack and whose head sat upon that mountain of flesh like some pagoda upon a mountain peak. He was slit-eyed, well greased, yellow and watchful. His fingers itched for the bribe I gave him. His name was Yang T'ang, a crazy singsong thing.

He escorted me into the presence of the Princc.

The Prince of East Sung was a very young man with a smooth yellow complexion, more Chinese than Mongol. He wore a beautifully embroidered blue gown and a small round cap and a pair of cavalry boots with golden spurs. He leaned back in his massive blackwood chair as though too weary to even think about moving.

"You have come," he said in a bored voice, "for my protection. You cannot have it."

I had not spoken and his refusal of a request I had not thought to make took me off balance.

"I am here," he continued in Oxford English, "because my ancestors were here. But my subjects desert me and join me at will. I have a personal bodyguard but the cavalry you have seen is not mine; the cavalry only wishes my protection for the moment and attaches allegiance to me only as long as they think they need my support. So do not ask for aid, *Tou-kie.*"

He was not being encouraging. He had called me "foreign dog." But it sounded so odd, those drawling broad A's coming from that mouth, I could not help but smile. "So doah not ahwsk foah aid."

From my pocket I produced a hundred dollars in Bank of Taiwan notes. I laid it respectfully upon the dais. He glanced at it and then at the captain who had brought me in. The captain was licking fitfully at his gross lips.

"That is better," said the Prince. "Since you request nothing, I will give you the escort. The country, I might add, is dangerous. But what do you want? Old bones?"

Incautiously, I said, "Gold."

He sat up stiff as a poker, staring. "Gold? Here in Mongolia? *Tou-kie,* you are a fool among fools. Go back to Peking and forget about this thing."

"No, you do not understand," I insisted. "I merely wish to try out the old streambeds of the region, to prospect that which has not been touched before. I take no wealth from the people, but from the land where it has lain forgotten."

"Escort him out, Yang T'ang," said the Prince with a disgusted wave of his hand. "Think well about this, *Tou-kie,* or you may find gold."

That was not encouragement, as I found out later. That was a threat, a threat more ugly than any I would ever hear again. He had, with that remark, sentenced me.

Yang T'ang led the way outside. "I am going north," he said in broken English. "My men and I will ride with you."

"I will pay you well," I replied.

"Think nothing of the pay," said Yang T'ang. He was being big-hearted. He wanted it all in a lump when we got beyond the ridges which surrounded the palace.

Did I find gold? Yes, of course I found it, but under conditions different than anything I had ever before encountered, and in a setting which Dante might have envied.

Gold? A river of it, certainly.

But I did not suspect these things. My mind was too orderly to even dream of them. I rode, that morning, with Yang T'ang.

CHAPTER TWO

ON the third day, riding north along the great caravan route which was nothing more than camel tracks in the caked earth, we sighted a column of riders who suddenly appeared like so many black dolls along a ridge two miles or more to our left. The column stopped and inspected us and then closed in and began to ride parallel to us after the ancient fashion of Mongolian bandits.

Yang T'ang was agitated and surly. He saw his spoils going away from him into the hands of those riders.

"That is one who calls himself Biki," snarled Yang T'ang. "Maybe so a Tartar, but just a cutthroat bandit. He says one of his ancestors was a general of Genghis Khan, but I have my own ideas of the identity of his father."

We were all strung out when this man Biki first appeared. Now Yang T'ang's men began to bunch up as though for common protection. They rode warily, hands upon rifle stocks, eyes flickering over the terrain and then back to Biki and his men.

We had thirty soldiers with us, all of them looking like bears, wrapped as they were in their sheepskin coats and topped by their fur hats. Our mounts were shaggy Mongolian ponies, small but strong, hammerheaded, hard-jawed and longhaired.

Although the weather was down to freezing and perhaps below, the wind which whipped and howled about our ears was filled with dry, stinging dust. In this country it never snowed. Is there anything worse than cold dust?

We were covered with it until we turned the color of it and I was as yellow as the next man.

I took my field glasses and inspected this Biki, and at a thousand yards I could see him with great clarity in spite of his coats and equipment which made him look like a mound in the saddle. Biki had a thin face and eyes which looked like silver slivers. His mustache was patterned after the great conquerors, a thin, lengthy thing which stood out straight over his almost lipless mouth. You expected him to clatter like a skeleton.

He had fifty-four men with him. I counted them, one by one, all strung out one after the other, each one looking like the last, each one wearing a padded coat and a fur cap, each one carrying a rifle of one make or another, anything from Sniders to Mannlichers, from .22 caliber to .50.

They looked like a capable crew, ready for anything.

Yang T'ang muttered, "He has done this before, *Tou-kie,* and I am growing weary of it. Every time I get something good he has to come and try his hand at me and it matters not how many times I beat him off. But this time he has more men than I. Tell me, *Tou-kie,* can you shoot? I see that you have a good rifle there."

Indeed he saw that I had. The rifle was a cut-down sporting Springfield, shooting extra-velocity dums. His eyes were covetous for the weapon.

"A little," I replied.

"Unfortunately," said Yang T'ang, "my men have little ammunition and perhaps it would be best for us to run while there is yet time. This Biki, although I am the braver man, always makes me uneasy. He is a good fighter, *Tou-kie.* His men all think that they are *bagaturs.*"

I had been looking for something like this to happen. Bandits were too common in the land, and I had no reason to become involved in the feud of Yang T'ang-Biki.

It occurred to me then that Yang T'ang would not worry about running away. He was worried about losing me, a valuable prize. And it also occurred to me that this Biki might well have picked up the information that a rich *tou-kie* had gone upcountry looking for gold. News travels very fast in that land.

I felt like a valuable, inanimate object which lies upon a gaming table waiting for the next throw of the dice.

"*Tou-kie,*" said Yang T'ang, in a pleading voice, "you are a better shot than we are and you could doubtless hit one of those men without half trying. Supposing you dismount and try your luck?"

It was an order and although I was unwilling to be made the goat, I drew in and swung out of the crude, crosstree saddle and drew the Springfield from its boot.

"The range is too long," I said, adjusting my sights. "But I'll give them a clip."

Through the sights, a horse and rider looked no larger than a pinpoint; a thousand yards was a considerable range.

It did no good to sight in on it. I had no way of marking

the bullets in the dust. In sling, prone, I let them have five as fast as I could fire.

Of course I hit nothing, but they must have heard the bullets sing. They split up and spread apart like an unfolding hand of cards.

Then the returning salutation came our way. The far-off shots sounded hollow and thin. *Cough-pang, cough-pang.* To the right and left small spurts of dust went up.

I might have done better than to fire that clip as I later found, but it was done. I swung up again and we started out at a trot toward a pass which was opening up before us.

Biki's horsemen strung out in a line of black periods and started to head in toward the same place.

Our trot became a run and the drumming of hoofs grew louder and quicker in our ears. I laid on with a quirt and we began to devour the intervening miles.

Biki was hard by us, drawing closer and closer. It was the path or nothing. The first man there would have all the advantage. He could hold the narrow entrance indefinitely, even with knives.

As we ran our excitement mounted. We began to yell and flay our mounts. The dust rolled back like a thundercloud, yellow as a typhoon. The plain raced under us in a blur. The bitter wind cut marrow-deep through our furs.

I knew, before we had gone a mile, that this was going to be serious. Once up there, if Biki got there first, we would meet a blazing scythe of fire. And if we got there first, Biki would be mowed down.

The weaker horses began to drop back. Yang T'ang and I

were racing side by side. We had the best ponies of the lot. So intent were we upon reaching that pass that we did not look behind us.

Genghis Khan himself could have done no better than Biki did upon that occasion. Timur the Limper himself would have been pleased by such an exploit.

Under the cover of their dust cloud, half of Biki's riders were dropping far to the rear, cutting over at right angles to get behind us.

Yelling into the icy knives of the wind, we did not realize that we were caught in the jaws of a bear trap. Twenty-five or more men were coming up, unseen in our own dust. The rest of Biki's force, upon the fastest mounts, was racing into the pass.

If Biki made it before us, we could not turn, but we did not know that and our quirts lashed the harder and our faces were beaten into raw red by the buffeting wind as we rode.

Another mile and Biki was gaining upon us. We were both riding at an angle and the distance we had to travel was the same.

And we did not notice that half of Biki's men had disappeared.

To me this was a minor affair, an exciting break in the monotony of the Gobi. I did not care about a fight, I welcomed it. Something warming in a fight and the desert was so cold. But I was to realize my error in a short while. This was going to come close to costing me my life and liberty forever.

We saw, suddenly, something which Biki must have seen before us. We had to cross a dry gash twenty feet deep in the plain and Biki had nothing but hard desert pavement before him.

The gash opened like the Sunken Road at Waterloo. Our men, not seeing, pressed ahead with slack rein and busy quirt. Yang T'ang and I, side by side, took the brink in a despairing leap, too late to stop.

I expected my horse to crumple under me when he hit, to break his legs and then roll me under grinding hoofs.

But the gravel at the bottom was loose and it acted as a spring cushion. Twenty feet down and my horse only paused in his stride long enough to regain his imperiled balance.

Beside me Yang T'ang took it and behind us the thirty came over like a yellow, roaring avalanche, undaunted by the danger of being trampled to a lifeless mess.

In that instant I knew why these people had once conquered all Asia with a handful. The gift of carelessness was still with them.

Up the side of the gully we thundered and then out again into the open plain. But Biki had gotten ahead of us, too far ahead for recall.

But Yang T'ang, once started, could not now draw back for fear of losing face, and onward we plunged, racing a race which was already lost and won, not knowing that behind us came a force nearly as numerous as our own. Damn that dust which obscured them.

Biki raced into the pass and wheeled, dismounting his men as fast as you can blink your eyes, throwing them behind rocks and into niches with sheer physical strength.

We tried to charge, spread out in a fan. Before us rifles

opened up with a cymbal crash. Snake tongues of scarlet lashed at us from under the yellow pall.

A man screamed and went down. A horse rolled over, shedding its rider who was quickly mounted on the fallen Mongol's horse. We reared and spun about and started to race back.

But from the gully we had just left came the spiteful crash of a withering volley. The air turned alive about our heads. Another man went down, two more horses.

We again tried to get out by darting toward the open plain upon our left but suddenly a charging mass of horsemen raced out of the gully and out of the pass and flanked us.

We met them with a crash which made the earth tremble. Short swords were bright in the sullen day. Men were crowded together in a tangle of horseflesh and dust which defied description.

A Mongol loomed beside me, lance ready for a thrust. I snatched at my .45 and stabbed him through with acrid flame. He had no more than dropped back, dying in his saddle, then he was replaced by another.

A rifle exploded almost against my face. My horse had reared in time. I fired again and again into the press about me. Men fell away, dissolved into the saffron fog. I knew not right from left nor friend from foe until I saw Yang T'ang.

His great bulk loomed beside me for an instant.

"Ride!" he bellowed, pointing.

I set in my spurs and rode. Magically I came out of the fray on the open plain. Cracking down with my quirt I streaked out toward the far hills. Men were about me, running with me. I thought in that frenzied moment that I had gotten away and that Yang T'ang was with me.

But he was not. Yang T'ang was gone, the gods of Mongolia knew where.

I stabbed a look behind me and there, close upon my blurring, rattling heels, I saw the thin, bony face, the colorless eyes of Biki.

He was grinning as he yelled for his men to come on.

I was the game and they were the hounds. I was the pawn for which they had been fighting.

The yelling cavalcade drew abreast of me on either side. Shots rapped harshly about me. They did not want my carcass, they wanted my money.

Head down, gagged with despair, I rode.

The yelling cavalcade drew abreast of me on either side. Shots rapped harshly about me. They did not want my carcass, they wanted my money.

CHAPTER THREE

IF ever Ichabod Crane fled from the Headless Horseman, he would have had to travel very fast to even keep up with me. Those Mongols were the direct descendants of the Khans who had built pyramids of human skulls to mark their conquests all over Asia. They were yellow-fanged demons astride fire breathing mounts. Their slitted, blood-colored eyes were merciless. They wanted nothing but my money, and perhaps, before I died, they would amuse themselves by making my last minutes pass with exquisite agony.

The whole horizon rocked and blurred before me. My mount, thank God, was fast and wiry, not easily tired. I had fed him with grain and those of the Mongols had been fed with grass.

But the plain was treacherous and footing was insecure and at any moment I might go thundering down, to be pounded to hamburger under the rolling hoofs of my pursuers. They were horsemen far better than I would ever be. They had been raised in those forked saddles and they could put the Cossacks to shame with their riding.

The yellow flow of ground beneath me was encouraging. If I could keep it up . . .

The spiteful crack of their rifles was drawing slowly away.

They could hit nothing from their saddles, but there was always a chance of a spent bullet. They must have thought me very rich—but then, to the Mongol a *tou-kie* is always rich—to go to all this trouble.

A range of hills rose before me. Somebody had taken a huge sword and had hacked away all their peaks, leaving so many rough tables standing in this sullen expanse.

I took heart. I might be able to make cover and dive in and take a chance with my rifle. Biki saw it too and the yells of his men grew louder and more fierce. They sounded like howling wolves about to close down upon a luckless stag.

Dangerous country, had said Charlie Martin. He had been right. But this was minor and it was annoying and it didn't fit with my plans at all. This was merely some skirmish which I might be able to escape and when I did I would probably forget all about it.

So I thought. How wrong I was! Something worse than death was waiting at the hands of Biki and his hellish crew. And Yang T'ang wasn't dead. Oh, no, he wasn't dead. I would meet him later on and what a surprise I would get. And the Prince of East Sung, that indolent young man with the Oxford accent, what would he say to all this in his region?

I decided, rolling across the plains, that it was about time Japan did something to settle up this land. I would speak to somebody about it.

Yay, speak to somebody, with death riding there at my stirrup, and worse than death. Queer, the importance men attach to their influence and their thoughts at such a time.

A ravine was opening up to me, and as I rode, the angle by which I approached made it appear that the very walls were folding back in welcome as though they were some great gate.

A huge boulder lay to the left of the entrance. I fixed my hopeful gaze upon it and slid the Springfield out of its boot, getting it ready for the fight which must ensue.

Only half checking the speed of my mount, still gripping reins and rifle, I flung myself off and went hurtling headlong through the dust like a toboggan.

Whirling I thrust the rifle's blue snout over the edge of the rock and took a quick potshot at the nearest rider.

Biki's outfit had checked its pace. They were less than two hundred yards away and coming broadside in an attempt to curve away.

Hastily I reset my sights. Once I had been good at this sort of thing and I prayed that the knack would not desert me now.

Five smoking bullets whipped into the mass of horsemen. Five glittering empties came clattering out to ring on the echo-tortured rocks.

Two men came down. A horse reared and went straight over backwards, its rider struggling clear with a leap like a cat's.

Another clip and another close, fast fusillade. Another man, another horse. My range was good and the targets were many. My rifle was far better than any of theirs. When my slugs hit I knew, from their effect upon game, that they tore holes a sparrow could fly through.

The Mongols drew off hastily, leaving their dead and wounded upon the field behind them. I gave them a third and parting clip. Their forte was horsemanship and they couldn't stomach the fire from such a rifle. They had better ways of getting me than allowing themselves to be killed.

Far better ways.

More satisfactory to their blood lust.

They did not stop until they were a thousand yards off. I wasted no more bullets, fully expecting a charge. For half an hour, they clustered about Biki, evidently talking excitedly, making their plans.

It seemed reasonable that they would wait for the rest of their number to come up and then get into the hills and flank me. That was the plan as I mapped it out.

But after a long time, when they had done nothing in that direction, I realized that they had another scheme in mind. Whatever that was, I could not even guess, and I took heart in the knowledge that in the darkness I could slip away. A man is hard to find in the Gobi.

Very shortly after I had concluded that they would attack no more, they rode away, heading west and away from me as though no longer interested in anything I did.

I stood up and caught my pony and took a drink of water from my canteen. I was grinning about it because, it seemed to be, I had outsmarted them once and for all.

I sloshed the contents of the canteen with assurance and then, after a moment, listened intently to it. Fool that I was, I had drunk heavily of my water that morning. I was almost out. And of food I had none. It had all been in the packs with my gasoline dry panner, my maps and my personal effects.

But I had my rifle and I had my sample pick and I had a horse. I would have to let things take care of themselves and receive whatever the Mongolian gods offered me, a foreigner, a *tou-kie,* in their land.

I went on up the ravine and found that shelves of rocks made good walking. I left no tracks and carefully turned on my own trail several times, working higher into these flat-topped hills. Far ahead of me, rising like some giant's store of brown sugar, I could see a mountain which really had a peak. It was the lord and master of all the others. Lacking another goal I made for this, stopping every mile or so and climbing up to higher ground to make certain that I was not being followed.

I did not know what had happened to Yang T'ang and I must admit that I didn't care too much. That cutthroat had had his eye on my equipment all the time anyway, thinking to knock me off as soon as we were far enough into the Gobi and away from the Prince of East Sung—who might possibly be interested.

That night I found a cave and managed to lead my suspicious pony into it for shelter. Carefully, I covered up all the outside tracks. I hung the doubled saddle blanket over part of the door to help keep out the wind and felt myself reasonably safe, even to the point of building a small fire which, though its smoke blinded and choked me in those close confines, at least drove away some of that terrifying chill of the howling wind.

I kept guard most of that night, sleeping only fitfully. In

the dark hours I knew that I was not yet safe from Biki. He would want vengeance now after I had killed some of his men and vengeance he would have. I knew that Biki would enjoy sending me to hell, and the upshot of it was that he did.

In the morning, with everything chill and gray, I started again for the mountain I could see in the distance. It seemed reasonable that I would reach it about noon, but something occurred which threw off my plans again.

I traveled until about ten o'clock. The sun had forgotten to come up and had sent a yellow, glowing haze of dust to take its place. Everything was yellow and even my horse had jaundice, so it appeared. And the wind howled as it has howled since the beginning of time, bringing down the bitter winter chill of Siberia and the North Pole. Nothing was in its way to stop it for a thousand—for two or three thousand—miles north. The wind tries to blow like that in Texas, but it hasn't the same biting viciousness of the cold, dry plateau.

My furs were not enough to keep me warm and I wished for a better clime, wished very ardently for heat. The Mongolian gods must have heard me.

At each new ravine I expected to meet Biki or his scouts. I was uneasy as though I trespassed where I did not belong. I felt an ugly premonition that all was far from well.

But when I arrived within a few miles of that mountain I made a discovery which drove all other thoughts from my brain.

Passing along a gully which might once have been a stream I saw that whole sections of the bed were black. That meant iron and other minerals. I was always upon the watch for that. I dismounted and got out the short, two-purposed sample pick and began to peck at the rocks as I walked, as an engineer will.

The rocks were not mineralized and I began to realize that the source of this stream must be the source of all this black sand.

Finally my curiosity got the better of me. I took a small iron pan I always carried and began to work over a few handfuls of the streambed. It was tedious because it was necessary to blow along the edge, slowly and laboriously, washing out the finer dust, exhausting my lungs and making my mouth dry and my lips chapped. I had seen the Indians of Mexico do that but I had never thought my own breath good enough until now.

The result, though long in coming, was worth the wind. In the bottom of that pan, standing out like twin jewels, were two "colors" the size of a pinhead. Mere flecks they were but they showed that I was right.

God forgive my excitement when I found out that these things were gold.

Raw gold, never before seen by any man but myself, lying there in the rough pan, virginal and bright.

I yelled with glee. I tried another pan a little higher and found three colors, unaware of the fact that the day was passing and that my thirst had grown unbearable. Nothing meant anything but that gold, and that the farther I went the more I found.

Finally I stood up and stared at the mountain ahead. The stream came from there. Perhaps this was the thing of which I had always dreamed. A mountain of gold, lost in the Gobi.

Little did I know that I was staring straight into the gaping maw of hell.

CHAPTER FOUR

AS a lodestone draws a needle, so did that mountain draw me. I was aware of a certain geological incongruity from the first. The surface of the earth here was secondary sedimentary formation, as is the greater part of the gigantic saucer which is the Gobi, or the Shamo (Sand) Desert. Gold is found mainly in primary formations, or rather in formations which were madc at the time the earth was still molten and have not since been changed.

But gold, according to mining men, is where you find it, and I had found it here.

I went on toward the mountain without knowing its identity. I knew I was in the northwest section of the Gobi and that a large mountain really had no business to be here, but on I went, stopping to test.

It was almost sunset when I made my way to the foot of that tawny peak. I stared up at it, and in the yellow rays of the dying sun, it looked like some great pile of the precious metal. And then, when the sun went lower to the dusty horizon, the whole mass turned crimson, as though it had been painted in blood—an evil omen at best.

Wandering along the foot I at last heard a sound which I took to be the wind sighing and moaning as it compressed itself through a defile. The sound was monotonous and ugly and had a depressing effect upon me. I did not consciously follow it, but at last I heard, coming from its depths:

"Om mani padme hum. Om mani padme hum."

Lama priests! That idiotic chant, meaningless and ageless: "Jewel of the lotus flower."

Low at first, then high and rapid and then low again, always the same, never changing its solemnity. Now and again I heard the croak of a bull fiddle and the roar of a forty-foot horn.

What was this, up here lost from the world? Some weird Lama rite? Some forgotten monastery?

I worked myself up to higher ground so that I could look back into a small depression in the mountainside. There I stood, frozen by the wind and by terror.

Bathed in the scarlet rays of a cauldronlike sun, half a hundred priests were sitting in a semicircle in the natural amphitheatre.

Each shaven head was bowed, each greasy yellow cloak was motionless. Half a hundred throats chanted, *"Om mani padme hum."*

If ever I have felt a sense of evil it was there. Ugly tales had come out from the world about these people. Their sacrifices and their stolid tortures had sent but few captive travelers back to civilization. They were, of course, supposed by the governments to be harmless enough. These Lamas controlled the religion of the Mongolias and played their part in politics. But few cared to delve deep into their rites.

For minutes I stood there simply because I couldn't tear my eyes away. Any moment one of them might look up and see me against the sky. With a great effort and with a feeling that everything was wrong, and mentally kissing my gold goodbye, I crept down to my horse and mounted, turning his head into the south.

I rode through the twilight with the wind slashing at me and howling through the crags, thinking and paying very little attention to the ravine walls on either side of me.

It was because of this that I walked straight into the troopers of Biki.

One moment the gorge was empty and the next I was confronted by a solid wall of horsemen blocking my way, quietly sitting their mounts, looking at me and saying nothing. The crying of the wind said enough.

Startled, I jerked up on my reins and wheeled. Behind me the ravine was blocked by other motionless horsemen. They had come like ghosts through the noisy darkness and now they merely sat their mounts and waited.

My hand slipped to the butt of my .45 but came away. I would be killed the instant I drew. Cut off from any retreat I had to gamble with the none-so-tender mercies of a Mongolian cavalry chief.

Biki detached himself from the horsemen and came forward. From the rank behind me came another man. Two or three quick motions removed my weapons from their holsters.

Biki, with mock courtesy, saluted me. He spoke, I was amazed to note, English comparable to the Prince of East Sung's.

"You have come far," said Biki. "I think it would be better for you to rest for a while—a long while."

His narrow, ugly face was impassive but his slitted eyes suggested a cruel humor.

"You've got me," I replied. "I suppose you'll shoot me and take my money and that will be that."

"Oh, no," said Biki. "I will take your money but I certainly shall not shoot you. You killed four of my men. You are worthy of a better fate than mere shooting."

"Cat and mouse," I said. "Get it over with."

"You came into this country for gold," said Biki. "Oh, I know all about it. Yang T'ang was full of information and I had it before he spoke. You came for gold, *Tou-kie,* and you shall find it. Plenty of gold. I myself will see that you are taken to the place where you can best discover it."

I was in no mood to fence with words. He meant something very vicious, I could tell that by the languorous drawl he affected.

"Have patience," said Biki. "I am fortunate that I found you this night." He sang out a command and the soldier who had disarmed me now began to relieve my person of all its valuables. Biki laid my money belt across his saddletree, not bothering to look into it.

He cried another command and his men took my reins and began to lead off, back toward the mountain. I was mystified by the move, but I said nothing. The soldiers in the darkness rode silently, their unshod ponies making no sound in the soft sand which had drifted into this ravine.

After a while a sound drifted down the wind and blended with it. Again I could hear that monotonous chant and the croak of great fiddles and the roar of the horns.

We were going back to the Lamas!

I looked sideways at Biki. He smiled and said, "You came for gold, you will get your gold. The gods of the Gobi are kind, *Tou-kie*."

He gave that last word a Chinese inflection and I knew that he meant it to mean another thing, "insolent dog." It contained a great deal of meaning. I had been too bold coming up here and I would pay the price. God knew what I faced.

At last the cavalcade drew into the amphitheatre. A great fire was burning and I wondered where they had gotten sufficient wood until I saw a man come forward with a bucket of black fluid and throw it on.

Crude oil!

For an instant the mining engineer in me was uppermost. But Biki was beginning to talk, still mounted, to the assemblage, though I could not gather what he said, having no knowledge of the Mongol tongue—that many-sided thing.

Biki kept pointing toward the mountain and down.

A shaven-headed, greasy-robed priest came up to Biki's stirrup and Biki got down in reverence. They spoke together in low tones and then the priest turned to the crowd and began to talk in a twanging singsong.

His remarks were interspersed by *"Om mani padme hum"* and the clatter of a prayer wheel. The leaping tongues of the fire painted them orange and black and the wind whimpered and moaned through the wastes, an undertone to the chant.

I had the feeling of unreality, that this thing existed only as a nightmare and would soon vanish. But it did not, and at last the priest bade the soldiers lift me down.

Another Lama came forward carrying a chain in his two hands held before him. I recoiled from it but two soldiers and Biki thrust me ahead.

Other priests came up and the chains were quickly fastened to my wrists and to my ankles. The clanking black harness had still another lead, a coupling, and I could guess what to expect from that.

Biki wanted unending revenge for the death of his men. He was getting it even now.

CHAPTER FIVE

AT last the chanting died down and from behind the rocks I could hear more chains. Into the firelight came a line of beaten, dismal prisoners, most of them Chinese, all of them with bowed heads, bearing the brand of whips, most of them naked and chilled blue by the cold.

From another section of the amphitheatre came another line, clanking and staggering beneath the weight of the iron. At its head I saw a familiar figure although he was now stripped of his furs and though his body was lined with black gashes.

Yang T'ang was leading his own men for the last time. His head was erect and his great body almost swaggered. He glared about him at the priests.

Yang T'ang saluted Biki with an insolent epithet and Biki smiled. I knew then that Biki had taken the other prisoner and, in payment for past trouble, had turned him over to this unholy crew.

I was coupled to Yang T'ang as one ox to another. Greedy hands stripped off my furs and the wind began to gnaw through my bones. A whip whistled and cracked. White flames of agony ripped through my body.

Then from the midst of the priests came a prancing, sidling

figure. A grotesque horror which, although I knew it to be a masked man, struck terror through me. The firelight was held by a human skull which tipped the end of his scepter. The man, all in black, even his head, was merely a shadow carrying that wand of horror.

He was, and I did not need to be told, the priest known to all Mongols as "The Prince of Hell."

From other portions of the clearing came other men, wearing stags' heads in which great jewels glowed between the horns. They capered about us. In their hands they held great clots of red and I knew that they carried dripping human hearts, either made up for the occasion or terribly real.

These were the devils.

The horns and fiddles began to blare, drowning out the wind. Whips sizzled and exploded upon chilled flesh. The beaten prisoners began to move forward, shuffling, chains clanking.

We were moved in toward the mountain. The priests cried loudly after us and then, suddenly, the horns were silent and the chant was again taken up.

"Jewel of the lotus flower. *Om mani padme hum.*"

That was the last dismal thing I heard. After that, silence. No wind, nothing but the clank of a chain. The Prince of Hell led on, and we saw ahead, in the gloom, a great ragged hole in the mountainside.

The devils fell away from us. Men came up on either side, seemingly through solid rock, and took their places on our flanks. The Prince of Hell led on, his skulled scepter swinging back and forth.

Smoking torches lit our way, throwing a grim light over the flayed backs of the prisoners.

It came to me then that I was condemned to hell. Something of this had reached my ears down there in China. The Mongols had a hell and the priests sent men there. This was it.

Our steps began to lead down and ever down. The chains clanked and the torches flickered and the Prince led on, down and ever down.

Our path began to curve to the left and it became steep. Odd smells came to me, reminding me of sulfur and brimstone, though that could not be.

With an effort I rescued my reeling senses. I was a man of the twentieth century, a trained mining engineer, and all this was easily explained. The Mongols tried to work upon the superstitions of their people by this simple mechanism.

Back in the thirteenth century a man known as Aloadin, or Hasan ibn Sabbah, who led a group of men popularly known as the Assassins, had caused to be built a tailor-made paradise, complete down to rivers of honey and milk and the dark-eyed houris, the better to control his followers. The Mongols, quite evidently, had manufactured themselves a hell.

I was a mining engineer and I had no right to let this strike terror into me. This was a subterranean passageway, eaten out by ancient rivers which had connected lava bubbles. The mountain might be hollow, as many mountains are. This was just another Luray Cavern or Mammoth Cave. It went down into the earth as other caves have done. Softer rock had been washed from harder rock. I could even see the signs of erosions and the faults occasioned by forgotten earthquakes.

Yes, it was all very simple, but even Yang T'ang cringed.

With the Soviets usurping their ancient commands, the Mongols were again trying to gain control over the superstitious peoples. The Lamas, with the help of Japan, were again establishing their rule in Mongolia.

But down, down, down we went, and the air began to stifle us and the torches licked upward at the blackened walls of the wide tunnel and the path still went down.

I lost count of the miles we walked. I knew that most of the world's great caves had not been fully explored and that they might reach miles deep into the earth. I had learned that from my mining books.

But unreasoning terror, fighting down all logic and knowledge, told me that I was going down into the bowels of the earth, that I was, in truth, bound for hell. That I would never see the sun again and there would be no trace of my passing.

Whips and torches and march again. The clank, clank, clank of chains as we stumbled down the inclined way, curving and twisting.

It began to get warm and I forgot the chill of the Gobi. Warm? Why would it be warmer here than anywhere else? Were fires burning deep in the earth? Great cauldrons bubbling?

Or lava and molten metal?

I shook this foolish thought away as I stumbled on beside Yang T'ang. It was necessary to go deep before you felt the effect of the earth's inner mass. But, and a fact from a long-discarded text jumped at me, the heat of the earth under the intermediate layer was about a thousand degrees Fahrenheit. And that layer was from six to eighteen miles deep in many parts of the world.

As it grew hotter I realized that it was only necessary to get a mile below the surface to realize the effect of that molten rock and metal. One mile was hot at a mile deep in America.

What prevented some upheaval from bringing that layer closer to the surface of the outer crust? Nothing that I knew, especially in a region as badly faulted as this, showing numerous earthquakes.

Perhaps we marched toward some subterranean volcano, things not unknown in Asia. What had made this passageway through the earth, if not bubbling gas?

We had walked for two hours when I saw that the walls of the passage were greasy with black liquid. Cautiously I reached out and touched the side. I knew the smell. The whip behind me cracked and agony shot through me, but I knew what this was.

This was an oil seep and we were below the oil level. That bucket the priest had emptied upon the fire proved it. Below the oil level and still going down.

I began to sweat, both from warmth and worry. The temperature must be up to ninety and going higher. Foolish mortal that I was, how I longed for the searing cold of the Gobi.

Down, down, down into hell. Perhaps this was an age-old rite. Perhaps the Christian conception of hell came from this very place, passing through legendary annals and into the hands of the early Israelites. Certainly the conception came from somewhere and this must have been here at the time.

Three thousand years are nothing in geological time. Only man counts the years as lengthy.

It became too hot to breathe and I judged that we were not three miles under the crust of the world. I began, in that heat, to have strange ideas. All mineral was molten in the center of the earth, perhaps gold was here, an immense pool of gold, waiting only a ladle for the taking.

And then all logical thought left me. We rounded a last curve and came upon a grisly scene. We entered a great domed chamber too vast for description. Through it burned pots of crude oil, smoking and sending out a flaring, uneven light which made shadows dance along the rounding walls.

Men were working there, glistening with sweat, their bodies wasted to bags of bones. And as we approached, a Chinese worker fell across his pick, arms outstretched, rigid.

A naked, towering Mongol guard stepped up and kicked savagely at the taut ribs. With an annoyed snarl, the Mongol stooped down and jerked the man to his feet. The slanted eyes were wide open, already hardening. The guard threw the corpse back to the rocks and twitched his finger toward a pair of slaves, who bore the body down the chamber and pitched it into a swirling cauldron of flame.

Chained as we were, they thrust picks at us and pointed to the walls. We stumbled forward and dully began to work in the awesome light of the smoking cups.

My pick went deep on the first strike. A chunk of ore fell away and I saw it glitter as it went.

Not molten gold, but ore. And from the roof overhead

which supported three miles of earth, I saw pointed icicles hanging which glistened with beads of gold.

In that overheated chamber, working with the mercury up past a hundred and forty, barely able to move from the effect of the heat, I hacked my gold from the wall and watched it mount in a pile about my feet.

CHAPTER SIX

DAY and night were all the same. A man did not bother with time. He was too occupied with the heat and the muscle-grinding work, too exhausted to think.

There were no more than a hundred slaves there at the time. Slaves did not last long. Most of them were Chinese immigrants who had flouted the laws and customs of this country and, in payment for their crime, and to satisfy the thirsting vengeance of the Lamas against all foreigners, these Chinese were sent, as the Mongol phrase went, "into the depths of hell."

Brimstone and sulfur from the oxide ore, smoke from the torches, and before many shifts had gone by, the newcomers were as black as Nubians, greasy with sweat and filth.

We worked in chains, relieved only when the picks refused to rise and fall again. We were then given a sort of gruel and allowed to sleep in another chamber, still fettered.

Yang T'ang was defiant to the guards and his back attested that defiance was not the right attitude. In his sleep he moaned with the pain of it, but waking, his eyes were still arrogant and his mouth was set in a leer.

"Is there no way out of this?" I asked him as we rested.

"I have never heard, *Tou-kie,* that any man ever returned from hell."

"But what was your crime? Surely they'll let you out of here. You are one of them."

He shook his small head set upon his massive body without any neck at all. "I defied the wishes of the high command, perhaps the Dalai Lama himself. I do not know. Biki, condemn him, is the man responsible. I make no excuses to you, *Tou-kie.* But I intended to rob and murder you upon the afternoon we were attacked. This, in reality, has saved your life. You were nothing to me and I would not divide my spoil with Biki. Too often I have defied Biki and the commands of the Lamas. The Soviets have paid me for certain work from time to time and Japan wishes to take the country. Through the Lamas, Japan holds much power here.

"This land is divided against itself. The people think that Russia will save them, the priests think they can regain their power through Japan. They are returning to the old practices, as this sentence to hell will testify, in their attempt to gain control over the country.

"It matters nothing to me now who holds it. I have no allegiance to anyone except when I need money. Someday, if we ever get out of this, I intend to sweep this country of intrigue as a man sweeps a floor with a broom. I have my supporters, scattered as they are through the deserts. They are the last of the nomad Mongols and even yet we can fight.

"But no man would attack this place, even for me, certainly not for you. We are, in truth, in hell."

Lying there, weary and racked with pain, thirsty from lack of sufficient water, writhing in the suffocating heat which was rivaled only by Death Valley in midsummer and shriveled the flesh on the bones, I could not think without great effort. The irons had gnawed their way into my flesh and the wounds were festering with infection. Soon I too would be thrown into one of those blazing cauldrons where the ore was melted down. Soon I would be dead.

"Yang T'ang," I said, after a long interval, "you know that I am a mining man. I know about such things as this. They are getting out gold for some great purpose, much more gold than you suspect. This ore is running ten to twenty thousand dollars a ton. Why are they doing this?"

"Perhaps to finance Japan's campaign, perhaps to launch an attack against all men. Money buys anything."

"Except freedom here. We are surrounded with gold."

Yang T'ang stirred. "You say you are a mining man. That I believe. I have seen mining men before. I shall speak of it to the guard."

He did speak of it on the next shift and was knocked down for his pains. But the guard must have understood because they began to watch me carefully for any covert move on my part. They were suspicious of my knowledge, and after several eons of work, perhaps several weeks for all I knew, Yang T'ang told me that they thought it better to kill me lest I do something to injure them through my powerful magic.

Who was I to do anything? I was worn out, staggering, dying on my feet. Already three of Yang T'ang's troopers were dead and burned to ashes in the cauldrons. Others were almost gone. Only Yang T'ang and I remained really strong in comparison.

And then one day a string of new prisoners were brought

into the chamber. They were Chinese and Mongols, mixed. All of them were shaking with terror and when tools were thrust upon them they fell to work without the use of a whip. They were beaten already.

"Thieves from some prison," muttered Yang T'ang to me. "See, one of them has no right hand."

When the guards discovered this and found that this man could not hold a pick or push a wheelbarrow, they instantly fell upon him with knives. The body was thrown into the flames without comment from anyone. The work went on.

CHAPTER SEVEN

THE oil seep was almost half a mile up the incline from the chamber. We struggled after the broad-backed, cruel-faced Mongol guard with our burdens. How we would have relished crushing him to a splintery, dripping mass with those barrels!

But there was no chance of that. The Mongol had a short sword and a rifle and he was alert for any such move.

In the darkness driven back only by the sputtering torch, we arrived at the black, greasy section of the wall. Some man with more knowledge than the rest had drilled a small hole from whence came a thick, gurgling stream. It was not large and it took a long while for us to fill the barrels. The rest was welcome.

As I stood there, looking at the oil, I visioned the vast underground lake which must lie behind it. What wealth was here with this gold and this black oil. Millions of years ago, some great cataclysm had slaughtered millions of fish and animals and their bodies, mingled with plant life, had remained here under terrific pressure until they at last became petroleum. Under this layer was the original crust, containing the mineral wealth which we grubbed out under the lash of whips.

I said to Yang T'ang, "If I had a couple men for a while I could bring this oil right down to the chamber."

It was an idle thought, prompted by the engineering I had lived with so long. It seemed a shame that the oil would have to be carried by hand when it could run down by gravity.

The guard growled at us but Yang T'ang turned to him and told him what I had said. The guard stared at me and said nothing.

But when we had carried our heavy casks back to the chamber, the guard left us and talked for some time with the evident commander.

This was all that happened for the time. But many shifts later, three yellow-robed monks had Yang T'ang and I drawn to one side and conversed with me through Yang T'ang concerning my remark about the oil. Yang T'ang told them of my prowess at great length, but I cared little about what was said. Yes, I could feed the oil down in a ditch. No, it wouldn't hurt the oil. No, there was no danger. Did they think I would commit suicide by making it a danger? And how could I, besides?

The monks went away and after another dozen shifts or so, perhaps days later, when another string of despised workmen and criminals had been brought down, Yang T'ang and I were ordered to turn over our work to other men and begin on the ditch.

It was welcome, that order. It gave me a chance to use my mind again and it lessened the terrible labor to which I had been subjected.

Yang T'ang and I dug the ditch, half a mile long, and other

men lined it with flat tiles. But it appeared that I had been wrong. The oil, before it reached the chamber, seeped away.

In great anger the Mongols told me of this, and Yang T'ang made me understand that I had to do something about it. The heat sets a man's nerves on edge and I was hard put to keep from striking the guard. It would take time for the oil to soak its own way. Did they want everything in a minute?

"All right," I cried, "I'll give them oil." And knowing that Yang T'ang was the only one there who could understand me, I added, "Tell the twelve men you have left to come running when you call."

Yang T'ang told them. A host of Lama priests came to watch me work. They stood about on the incline, muttering and staring at me, their greasy yellow robes half black in the torchlight.

A guard cracked his whip and bade me to work and bring the oil along the ditch upon the pain of death. If I failed they would kill me. I knew that from their expression and their mutterings.

I demanded a hammer and a drill and then, as I had done so many times before, I began to single jack a hole into the wall above the first hole drilled so long before.

Silence hung behind me. The only sound was a ring of my hammer. I worked for minutes before I stopped. Nothing happened or could happen when I withdrew the drill.

They protested, and I told Yang T'ang to tell them, "This is slow magic. It takes much, much time. They will grow weary waiting."

The monks did not like this at all and they cried for my

blood. I would not use my knowledge to send the oil down into the chamber. They needed oil there and they needed the men who usually hauled it down in barrels. Oil must come. I began to curse the day I had made the statement that it could be accomplished.

I worked for hours, using longer and longer drills, making the hole bigger and bigger. The monks grew more restive. One of them argued in a high-pitched voice that I was cheating them and telling them lies and that I should be killed. So said Yang T'ang.

A diversion occurred when one of the monks remembered that there must be much gold down in the chamber by this time. Several of them, bored with watching me single jack, went down the incline.

After a long time I heard chains clanking below us and looked down. Because they were, by far, the strongest breed there, Yang Tang's men were coming up, staggering under their burden, carrying out the loot from the earth under the nagging whips of the guards.

They filed past me with not a glance, their chains clanking, their faces impassive. I heard them for a long while, still going up, as I worked.

And then I had a streak of luck. With less than twelve hours' drilling with hand drills, and with a hole less than eight feet deep, I struck a bubble.

The drill shot back into my face, knocking me down. A stream of oil under terrific pressure, less than half an inch in diameter but coming fast, sprayed itself against the opposite wall of the passage.

The Lamas scuttled with shrieks for cover and then, seeing that this did them no harm, commanded me to get the stuff into another ditch.

Weary and staggering, I started to do so. Yang T'ang worked beside me. The ground was slippery under our feet. In a few moments we had the connecting link and the oil began to streak down the ditch.

With a yell of childish glee, forgetting their cruelty for the moment, the Mongols ran abreast of it, staring at it, watching it gurgle down toward the chamber.

"Is that all?" said Yang T'ang.

I said it was and the guard began to again load us with our chains. He was the only man left with us.

CHAPTER EIGHT

WE had no plan. We worked spontaneously. Yang T'ang threw the man off balance. I brought up my length of heavy iron and smashed in his skull. He dropped without a sound and I twisted the bloody chains off my wrists.

Yang T'ang started to run but I called to him to wait. I had other plans, born of long suffering.

The stream of oil had started to hiss and although I could not smell it . . . Natural gas has no smell. I knew that the hole, wearing fast, was becoming larger and larger.

I took the sledge and crashed it against the wall, again and again. Yang T'ang helped with his chains. We battered the rock all about that stream, shocking it into cracking.

With an explosion which sent us both crashing against the far side of the incline, the gusher let loose. Gas and boiling black fluid came all out together with a mighty roar.

Deliberately, knowing exactly what I did, I sealed that chamber forever.

The fallen torch was all that I needed. I thrust it close to the outpouring stream. A roar and crash and a blinding flare knocked us down again. Blue and red flame came geysering straight across the passageway, blocking the exit with fire. And it would burn for years and the oil, going down, hot from the contact with burning gas, began to burn.

A sea of flame was flowing down into the chamber, to drown and fry every man there.

Yang T'ang grunted with satisfaction. Together we raced upward, away from that searing heat.

We were stark mad now, both of us, swinging our irons and yelling. The guards who had gone up with the chests were coming down again with the twelve soldier prisoners.

Suddenly the chained troopers wheeled sideways and Yang T'ang and I rushed in from the front. It was too easy.

We left those guards sprawled upon the incline, brains battered out of their skulls.

Up we went again, ready for anything. When we reached the upper side, we found a guard standing just inside the entrance.

The Lama soldiers whirled on us and began to fire. But we rushed on, the chained troopers dragging their unseparated dead with them. In a moment we had their guns.

Chains took the half dozen. The priests fled but we shot them down as they ran. We rushed out of the black hole of hell and found only horse holders to stop us.

Again we stopped and fired and again the field was clear. We hacked off our chains with hammers, mangling the soft iron until it broke. The chill wind was painful upon our overheated bodies and we stripped furs from the dead men and donned them.

We mounted then and started out. We took all the horses because we wanted no one to find them. We had left the bulk of this Lama order and the better part of its guards and soldiers to fry in the black hell of their own making, which I had changed into a very red and very hot hell indeed.

In the pack train we had the gold the twelve had brought up, and we had rifles, and we had our freedom. Nothing could stop us again. We were eleven in all, leaving three dead in the rush.

We headed north and west because that way we left the Gobi and all it meant. We were going deep into Russia and Yang T'ang knew that men with bags of gold would have no trouble getting through.

Our flight was uninteresting enough. We avoided the well-traveled ways and we came at last to a great city and our gold did what we wanted it to do.

Yang T'ang is somewhere in Siberia just now, with an army of his own. Occasionally Yang T'ang drops me a note in perfect English.

Recently he said, "Our friend Biki, *Tou-kie,* is very, very dead. He was unfortunately murdered in this town last week and his death was far from pleasant. I thought you would like to know."

And quite a while ago he wrote me that the Prince of East Sung is also dead. I know not what to make of that because Yang T'ang didn't bother to give me details. But the Prince of Hell . . .

But these things do not worry me. This set ring here is from the ceremonial cap of a Lama devil I looted from the packs. This bit of gold is part of my share which, so far as I know, is still intact down in Washington, waiting for gold to become legal again. Maybe when it does and you get a double eagle in your hands, just stop and look at the coin and wonder whether or not the metal might have come from a certain hole in the Gobi, which used to be called hell.

PEARL PIRATE

CHAPTER ONE

SMOKE ENGEL shook a violent finger under the yellow nose of Chan Tso-lan, the moneylender, giving the greasy fat Chinaman the full benefit of enraged gray eyes beneath unruly, straw-colored hair.

"You thief!" cried Smoke. "You knew damned well that copra was going down in price! That was why you were so fast to lend me money on the *Witch*. You think you can get away with anything down here in the Coral Sea, don't you? You think you can hang on to those loan papers, don't you? Cancel that debt, yellowbelly, or I'll make putty out of your greasy hulk!"

But Chan Tso-lan was bland and unmoved—he seemed round and inoffensive in spite of the evil glitter in his brown pig eyes. The Chinaman merely clapped his hands together and gazed about the room of his house above the lagoon.

"You will not pay, Mr. Engel?" The Oriental voice was heavy and sinister.

"No!" shouted Smoke. "And I'm not going to turn my schooner over to your thieving business, either!"

"Then," shrugged Chan, "perhaps you need a little persuasion." And he nodded toward the bulging curtains at the far side of the room.

Smoke stepped back and stared at the silken wall, and the move saved him a nasty wound in his side. A yellow arm shot out and flipped a deadly white streak of steel toward the American, and Smoke heard the twang of the vicious passage.

But before he could move to retaliate with the gun at his side, he felt the bite of steel in his arm and knew that another knife had been thrown at him from behind.

Chan smiled unconcernedly and retreated away from his desk out of range—and this, too, seemed to constitute a signal.

Yellow bodies, quicker than the eye, seemed to boil through the door toward Smoke Engel, and the ferocity of evil faces coiled about him with hard black eyes and jagged yellow teeth. Knives glittered with terrible light which seemed as alive and writhing as poisonous snakes intent on a kill.

Smoke struck out with a terrific right to a jaw and saw the man reel back, senseless. In that moment he knew two things. This was no mere "persuasion."

Chan fully intended to have him killed outright, for then, who would there remain to question the rightful ownership of the trim schooner which Smoke had long sailed about the South Seas?

Chan was not the only one who wanted possession of the *Witch,* but none so far had dared to face the strength and agility of the tall, lithe American. And death was a small thing here in this forgotten British outpost in the Coral Sea.

As he fought, the heat of the tropics coiled about Smoke as swift and deadly as the opponents, for a man could not long exert himself with the thermometer hovering around a hundred and ten—and the stench of unwashed bodies was sickening.

Chan's men were striving to hold Smoke's arms so that one

of their number could deal a fatal knife thrust to the American's heart, but Smoke had other ideas. His steel hands crashed into bone and flesh as swiftly and fatally as iron hammers.

With the sweat of exertion making his clothes sodden about him, Smoke brought one after another of the men close to him with one arm while he lashed out with a fist.

In the close quarters of the room it was difficult to find enough space to fight, and Smoke was afraid to back against the treacherous draperies which alone might have offered him some reprieve.

He was fighting now as he had never fought before, and the toll of his fists writhed upon the grass mat floor, grim warnings to the others.

A knife sank deep into Smoke's wrist, bringing forth a gush of scarlet blood which was not long in mingling with the blood drawn from his opponents. Red splattered dots stood out weirdly against sweating faces.

A man Smoke had knocked down now crept along the floor toward the weaving legs of the white man—and the intent expression on the battered face boded no good to Smoke—for once down on the grass mats, there would be little hope of victory for the white man.

Smoke heaved a body backward across the room with the speed and harshness of a pile driver, sending the Chinese crashing down into a rattan chair beside Chan, who dodged without changing expression.

The Oriental on the floor came closer, hitching himself forward painfully, to shoot out an arm as sinister as that of the slimy octopus. The yellow hand sought a hold on the white man's ankle that Smoke's balance might be destroyed and the fight ended.

But the hand never reached its destination. A pistol shot from the doorway cut into the melee like a knife, instantly silencing all combat.

Smoke whirled toward the opening, expecting to see one of his Chamorro sailors—but the man he saw was heralded to bring no succor. Smoke's gray eyes widened as recognition flashed across his face.

The hulk of dark flesh and matted black hair who held a smoking pistol silhouetted against the whiteness outside was a figure well calculated to strike terror into the heart of any Coral Sea trader or merchant. The infamy of Portuguese Joe Herrero, pearl pirate, lay as heavy and black upon the southern seas as a blot of ink upon paper.

The pearl pirate grinned thickly into the surprised faces before him and then shifted the pistol suggestively toward the victim of his announcing shot who sprawled hideously in a pool of red on the mat floor.

"Good afternoon, gentlemen," said Portuguese Joe in a silky voice. "I hope I have not interrupted your sport. Ah, yes, and Mr. Engel, I believe.

"You know, Mr. Engel, I have yet to thank you for the wonderful cargo of shell which you so kindly gave me last year. I did rather well with the shipment."

Smoke wiped a bloody hand across his mouth, leaving a dark smear and a salty taste against his lips. He opened his tight mouth to speak but snapped his jaws shut with a vicious click. The gray eyes had lost the light of battle and were now filled with a deadly hate which Portuguese Joe feigned to ignore.

Chan's expressionless face had suddenly become a blasted ruin of greasy terror and the Chinaman's heavy poise slid from him to leave a quivering, ugly, hateful being who groveled beside the desk.

Portuguese Joe cleared his throat noisily and spat upon the mats. "But there is little use in wasting time and effort upon ceremony. You, Mr. Chan Tso-lan, will please favor me with your bag of black pearls about which you were foolish enough to brag. And quickly!"

The Chinaman cast a sweeping look of despair at his frozen warriors and then began to babble that he had no black pearls.

But he had no more than mentioned the fact once when Portuguese Joe calmly sighted the chest of a stricken warrior and squeezed down on the trigger of his pistol. The shot blasted a gaping hole in the saffron chest of the man, knocking the lifeless body back with a hammerlike viciousness.

Those in the room cringed back and Smoke took an involuntary step toward Portuguese Joe. He thought better of the move and stopped.

Chan dived into a makeshift safe and brought forth a small white box which he threw fiercely at the pearl pirate—showing just once that he had some atom of defiance in his shriveled soul.

Portuguese Joe caught the box deftly and grinned, taking his eyes away from the room just long enough to see the eight black pellets which lay snugly in the cotton in the white box.

The pearl pirate gave the assemblage a brief bow and slowly backed away, deliberately turning about and showing them his back as he went down the road toward the harbor.

No one in the room moved, for they knew that unseen riflemen had the entire room covered—otherwise the pirate would never have been so brave as to show his back to foemen.

Smoke grinned mirthlessly at the prostrate Chan.

"You never can tell," he intoned, "when old Lady Fate is going to swap tables on you, Chan. And now that that is over with"—he drew his pistol slowly out of its flap holster and leveled it on the Chinaman, able to do so for the first time—"how about finishing our little game?"

Chan's head came up with a jerk and the pig eyes stared into the muzzle of the pistol. "Mr. Engel, I have something to ask of you." The voice was steady and expressionless, once more coming from the bland mask. "You are a fighting man and I have need of one just now."

"No tricks!" commanded Smoke with a brief gesture at the still-motionless warrior.

"No," said Chan, "no tricks! If you will get back those black pearls, I will give you the papers to the *Witch*."

"Huh!" sniffed Smoke. "You can fight your own battles, yellowbelly. I might have a score of my own to settle with Portuguese Joe, but that has nothing to do with you. Get me?"

Chan was disconcerted, but only for a moment. A greedy flame could be seen licking up in back of the brown eyes. "All right, Mr. Engel. I will give you ten thousand dollars cash on your return."

"Put it in writing!" snapped Smoke.

CHAPTER TWO

WITH a scrap of paper jammed into his dirty ducks, Smoke ran out of the hut into the whitely molten sunlight and poised for a brief instant to stare out across the blue lagoon.

He saw two ships anchored there—one of them the trim white *Witch,* swinging gently in an offshore breeze, the other a strange black craft, heavy under jet canvas above jet hull, which flew no flag and knew no law. Smoke started to run again, when he heard the rattle of anchor chains aboard the *Negrito.* He knew that the pirate ship would not be long in getting underway.

The Chamorro sailors of the *Witch* watched the approaching longboat which carried their captain, and black faces mirrored the singleness of knowledge which was theirs as soon as they saw the determined expression on Smoke's face.

As one man, the sailors turned about and stared after the departing *Negrito,* and then without further expression the crew ran to the halyards.

Smoke came aboard to the tune of hysterically rattling booms and chains.

With a strong brown hand on the heavy wheel, Smoke stood on the poop deck and watched the beach swing past the *Witch*'s bows as the trim craft came around to head for the open sea. A Chamorro came up on deck with an armload of machetes and rifles and Smoke nodded with approval as he watched the fellow distribute the arms to an eager crew.

There was no mystery in this avidity of the Chamorros for a fight. In the first place, they were some of the toughest specimens of Chamorros ever assembled on a deck, and in the second place, the crew of the *Negrito* consisted of Melanesians—men from the Solomon Islands. And between the two lay an age-old hatred which was forever fanning up with fangs of warfare.

The *Witch* lunged out into the sea swell as though she, too, were anxious to close with the black ship, and as the white bows clove the running sea the tenseness of taut booms and concentration and expectancy of battle fell over the entire assemblage like a cloud of red.

The *Negrito* had a lead of a full thousand yards, but the *Negrito*'s bottom was as foul as her crew and owner, and her heels were leaden when compared to the fleetness of her pursuer.

As soon as the two ships came in sight of each other, more canvas was seen to slither up the black ship's masts and the white froth of smashed seas boiled up higher under the black bowsprit.

Yard by yard the distance between the two ships lessened until, from either, the men on the other's decks were easy targets in spite of plunging, crazily canted decks.

A mad, hate-filled smash of rifle fire flickered up from both decks almost at the same time. Smoke turned over his wheel to a brown sailor to give a hand at the marksmanship.

He had no sooner quitted the post than the new helmsman tautened like a struck sword, driven lifelessly back by the cruel impact of a bullet in his side.

Smoke's expression did not change as he turned and waved another seaman to the helm.

Chamorros in the scuppers were methodically loading and firing at the fleeing black vessel and now and again a reeling dark figure on the *Negrito*'s decks proved that some of the shots were taking effect.

Smoke turned and gave a swift order to his helmsman and the *Witch* darted away on a new course which would eventually bring her directly abreast of the *Negrito.*

The sniping went on, more slowly now as the men settled to the business, and the two ships came together as the white schooner relentlessly closed the distance.

Chamorros broke out grappling hooks and huddled ready with them in the scuppers, while Smoke calmly counted the odds against him and sent brief cautions and orders along the gunwale.

The tactics he was about to employ had not been seen on the high seas since the days of Henry Morgan and Drake, and Smoke prayed that he might be at least a portion as successful as those two gentlemen rovers had been.

With a crashing grind of wood scraping wood, the two schooners slammed together. Grappling hooks clinked home to bite the two ships firmly together in an embrace which would only be broken by the death of either or both.

Machetes waved viciously under the gunwales as black arose to repulse a charging brown wave.

Dark faces were hideous in their hates, and white discs of fight-widened eyes stared straight into filed fangs as two races closed with each other to continue the battle which had gone on for thousands of years.

Smoke leaped up on a bitt and emptied his pistol into the howling black mob below him—and as he fired his last shot before hastily reloading, he knew that the odds were clearly against him.

It was too late to turn back now—and turning back had never found a place in Smoke's creed. And so he went on, though in rushing forth he was treading close upon the portals of death.

Machetes crashed on machetes and the spiteful barks of pistols and rifles blended into the terrific melee of shouting, screaming men. Hate, blood and death were as one on the deck of the *Negrito* as the scuppers began to widen out into a thick gush of red fluid.

Arms hung by narrow threads as machetes found their marks—hung or existed no longer. A head rolled away from the twitching, bleeding body of a Melanesian to come to rest against Smoke's leg as he stood and exchanged shot for shot with armed men on the black ship's quarterdeck.

Bullets whined off the bitts or cracked into suddenly collapsing bodies. The shrieks of hate were now intermingled with screams of pain as the deck became littered with wounded and dying. Now and then bodies slipped away into the sea, the slight gulf which still intervened between the clasped ships.

With his last cartridge gone, unable to attract the attention of his men for a direction of the attack, Smoke wrapped steel fingers about the head of a belaying pin and crashed his way aft toward the deckhouse where he knew Portuguese Joe must be.

So far in the fight he had seen nothing of the dark hulk, and the battle would be over with the death of one of the commanders. Smoke swiftly cut away a path through milling, death-locked bodies toward the short ladder which would surely lead to the cessation of the fight.

Bullets fanned close to his tan cheeks and powder stung his skin where it was exposed through his ripped clothing. The poop deck was a hotbed of powder flame where the hate-mad Melanesians were firing into friend and foe with appalling impartiality.

Smoke skirted an open hatch behind the mast and leaped up to the raised deck, his belaying pin held on high. A snaggletooth Melanesian, his breath terrible in the face of the white man, pressed a hot pistol muzzle into Smoke's ribs and jerked back on the trigger.

The white man darted to one side and brought the pin down with a force which carried it half through the face of his assailant. Failing to notice the bullet crease in his side, he leaped up to the top of the deckhouse and ran across black tarpaulins toward the wheel.

There was no thought now given to navigation, and the wheel spun unattended before the open companionway which led down into the cabins.

For a brief instant Smoke stopped tensely above the wheel,

a bloody scarecrow of a man, his muscled torso half bare through the bloody strip which remained of his shirt, the red-dyed brass of the belaying pin held in his stained hand, a wild, savage glare of battle making an awesome mask of his tanned face.

Oblivious to the snarls of hastily directed bullets which snapped about him, he threw back his shoulders, hefted the pin, and dived down through the companionway in quest of Portuguese Joe.

CHAPTER THREE

AS he reached the end of the passageway, Smoke plunged into the main salon utterly unheedful of the danger which might be coiling up to spring upon him in the dusky interior. It was only the swiftness of his motion which saved his life.

He had no more than bulked through the door, than the chattering death song of a machine gun licked out at him to send churning splinters away from the bulkhead he had just passed.

Without hesitation Smoke threw himself at full length on the floor of the cabin, clawing at the rug under his flattened hands in an attempt to heave himself forward toward the gun and to one side out of range.

A bullet hammered into his shoulder, sending him backward across the salon deck. Smoke glanced up to see the hideous, vengeful blotch against the skylight which was the contorted face of Portuguese Joe.

In that same glance Smoke saw the muzzle of the water-cooled machine gun dip down at him, saw the belt jerk as it fed the gun, saw brass cartridges spill out of the breech.

Slugs reached out with hot metal fingers to rip out the white man's heart, but Smoke rolled aside with the swiftness of a panther—a fraction of an inch ahead of the racing bullets which snapped a quick path across the rug, biting out gashes of fabric and wood at the rate of six hundred a minute.

All sounds within and upon these fight-maddened ships were suddenly concentrated in the crashing of the machine gun, and Smoke knew that his life depended upon getting past the arc limit of the tripod before Portuguese Joe, crouching wolfishly a few feet away, could swing the muzzle directly at the conspicuous, rolling target.

A scant arm's length away from Smoke, the gun's muzzle was searing him with powder in its attempt to stab him with lead. Though the odds were long against the success of the move, Smoke shot out a hand to grasp the crimson-hot barrel to stay the arc before it reached its fatal limit.

Though the steel burned the flesh from the bones of his fingers, Smoke held on and savagely thrust the barrel away from him.

Portuguese Joe, intent upon his marksmanship, was caught off guard and his ugly face was suddenly unmasked to show mingled terror and surprise.

He had been so confident that Smoke would at least attempt to bring him out of the salon and that the vicious weapon would do its work with appalling swiftness, that he had not once considered the possibility of defeat. And now that the thought sank down into him it momentarily robbed him of his strength.

An instant's inaction allowed Smoke to reach the pearl pirate's throat with a steel hand, allowed him to lurch up into a crouching posture which suddenly uncoiled into a spring, bearing Portuguese Joe back with the sheer ferocity of suddenly tripled revenge.

Disregarding his burns and wounds, Smoke held the man's throat in his strong hand and drove a sledgehammer fist into the dark features of the pearl pirate.

The blow would have been sufficient to kill any ordinary being, but the hard skull of Portuguese Joe only bruised the knuckles of Smoke.

Again the fist drove forward in a terrific punch and Smoke felt a bone snap in his hand. Before him he saw the blurred ugliness of the pearl pirate lurch upward, bringing Smoke with him.

Forgotten were the machine gun and clubs, for here was all the wild ferocity of beasts suddenly unleashed. Neither holds nor blows of any description were barred as the two swayed out into the center of the salon, locked in a savage clinch which did not restrain them from striking and gouging each other at the closest possible quarters.

They stumbled over the machine gun and were oblivious to it as it banged over on its side and lay dismantled on the floor.

Smoke pressed his thumbs into the other's eyes and with a roar of agony Portuguese Joe wrapped powerful arms about the other's slim body in an attempt to break Smoke's back.

In the musty dimness Smoke saw one of his thumbs sink home and felt, simultaneously, an agonizing twinge as he was relentlessly bent backward.

His senses reeled and he felt the other's evil breath against his cheek, saw a blur of bared teeth and snarling features.

Marshaling all his energy in one swift drive, Smoke doubled up a knee and sent the cap crashing into the dark one's groin. There was an instant of silence into which the howls from the deck came as a faraway nightmare. Then Portuguese Joe staggered back, doubling up, for an instant utterly helpless.

Smoke failed to recognize the strength of his enemy in that brief moment and he was caught off guard as his opponent straightened suddenly and crashed all his weight directly against Smoke.

With a shout of rage the white man gave ground, attempting to summon his strength quickly for another attack. But he was driven backward until he felt the door of the salon at either hand and knew that the bare wood of the passageway was under his feet.

Like an enraged bull, Portuguese Joe pressed his advantage with a force that was not to be denied and the thick, hairy arms strove to encircle Smoke for a clinch that would mean the white man's finish.

Smoke felt the ladder at his heels and stepped up, fighting off the arms, one step at a time, until the clear sky and the gathering night were all that remained behind him. He felt the wheel at his back and unwittingly stepped aside.

However enraged the pearl pirate might be, he was quick to conceive a plan which would mean a quick end to his assailant. Behind Smoke there now lay only a low rail and the terrible depths of the sea, and as he was forced rapidly back, Smoke realized his fate.

There was no escape now and he could only deal out blows and evade the clinging arms. Slowly he gave way toward the rail.

Smoke knew that within a minute's time he would trip over the rail, plunge backward, to be swallowed up by the waves. Even if he regained the surface, it was improbable that he would escape the vicious jaws of barracudas and sharks.

Over the shoulder of the charging Portuguese Joe, he could see the milling mob on the deck forward and knew that the battle there was as terrific as when it started. No eyes were turned aft, for all men were too busy parrying off blows and dealing death to their enemies.

Shots echoed through the ship and splinters splattered out where bullets bit into bulwarks and masts. The *Witch* still clung to the *Negrito* with iron hooks and Smoke knew that he would be victorious if he could only elude his assailant.

But getting away from Portuguese Joe was impossible and the flick of a second seemed an age when Smoke's heel touched the lower part of the rail and he felt it pressing against him, unbalancing him. In an instant he would plunge backward into the dark, greedy sea to vanish forever from the world of men.

In one last gesture of defiance, Smoke smashed a broken fist into the dark blur before him and saw blood spurt from the thick mouth. But however heartening it might have been to smash the pearl pirate's face, the move was fatal. With redoubled strength, Portuguese Joe drove Smoke up and over the rail.

CHAPTER FOUR

EMPTY space flashed about Smoke as he fell and though it was only a few feet down to the waves, he felt that the distance was infinite. Green-black froth curled about him as he plunged into the water which tore into his eyes and mouth, driving the life-breath from him, strangling him.

With mighty thrashings of arms and legs, Smoke broke his plunge downward and began to come back up to the surface. Hours seemed to pass before he again was able to fill his air-starved lungs on the surface.

Above him was the dark hulk of the black ship and beside that was the *Witch*'s stern, but between both ships and Smoke were things which writhed through the water with the ferocity of wolves ready to pounce viciously upon whatever the battle might offer.

Triangular fins were there by the dozen, attracted by the many dead bodies which already drifted about the bobbing, fight-racked ships. It was not the abundance of fins which caused Smoke to experience a twinge of terror. He knew what lay beneath the surface of the waves—barracudas with unseen death were waiting there ready to strike with the speed of light.

But Smoke did not wait for death to overtake him. He counted upon the presence of much meat to allow his safe passage to the rudder chains of the *Negrito*. A shark fin brushed by him and he kicked out in the water with one foot, meeting slimy resistance as the sea beast shot away to come back to attack.

Smoke struck out as calmly as possible for the rudder but he was unable to compel himself to forget the danger which swirled all about him. He felt a tug at his pants leg and knew that something had struck at him. He shot out his arms in a long stroke and scissor kicked, trying to ward off death as well as swim.

Then above him he could feel the waves hitting at the rudder and knew that if he could survive an instant longer he would be partially safe.

His hand caught hold of a chain and with a movement which was strengthened by the horror which surrounded him on every side, he swung himself up between the rudder and the ship, hastily dragging his entire length out of the water.

Teeth ripped at his trousers just as his legs left the water, and he glanced back to see the swirl caused by a six-foot barracuda whose two feet of teeth had barely missed dragging Smoke back into the sea.

Smoke saw that the rope of a longboat trailed over the stern into the sea and that, when the *Negrito* pitched, the rope swung toward him.

He stretched out and took three passes at the line before he could capture it. Then, with the rope held firmly, he looked again at the sea which licked at him. To swing away from the rudder meant placing his legs back in the water.

With set jaws and a tense motion of his body, Smoke

swung out on the rope, feeling the water beat at his shoes and expecting every instant that he would be pulled away from the line. As rapidly as possible he pulled himself up the rope, hand over hand, to breathe a sigh of relief when he was, at last, clear of the waves once and for all.

Cautiously he peered over the rail and down forward. The battle was quieter now, and the quarterdeck was deserted save for the dead.

The hulk of Portuguese Joe was moving toward two Chamorro seamen who stood back and hacked futilely into thin air with machetes, their strength robbed by the terror which had gripped them at their first sight of this apparition.

Smoke heaved himself over the rail and dropped to the sticky deck with catlike stillness. Weaving in and out between bitts and the wheel, he came to the top of the passageway which led down into the salon he had been forced to quit but a few moments before.

His face was a savage mask of determination as he ran down the ladder and into the cabin.

Wasting no time, he stooped over the sprawled machine gun and swiftly reloaded his cargo of potential death, making sure that the weapon was in readiness for the last scene of the fight aboard the *Negrito.*

Hugging the heavy gun to him, Smoke ran forward through the cabins and found himself ascending a ladder which must lead to amidships and whose door must command the entire deck and furnish protection at the same time.

With a kick he sent the door slamming open, and spreading

the tripod with almost the same motion, he set the machine gun down on the deck and quickly squatted behind its grim length.

Between clenched teeth he called out in the Chamorro he knew the Melanesians could not understand, "Lie down! Get to the port side of the ship. I'm going to fire!"

With the alien words whipping about them, the Melanesians dropped all holds and suddenly jumped stupidly back to stare at the afterdeck. They had understood no word that had been spoken and were not quick-witted enough to follow the example so swiftly set by Smoke's sailors.

Portuguese Joe whirled around and stared at Smoke as though his late assailant must surely be a ghost. But then the fighting energy within the dark hulk was too strong long to listen to the superstitious voice within him and he followed his animal impulse to charge.

Smoke saw the pearl pirate lunging forward and called out in English, "Stop! Another step and I'll fire!"

But the other paid no heed to the words. Brutality flicked savagely out of the brown pig eyes and the arms swung greedily at the man's sides. His steps were certain and unfaltering as he walked up on the gun.

"Stop!" shouted Smoke, and then saw that Portuguese Joe was so confident of his own strength and prowess that he thought himself invincible.

The chattering death song of the machine gun lashed out across the deck, seeming to come from between the strong hands of Smoke.

Portuguese Joe, twenty feet away, stopped, a startled expression gradually creeping up over his face. The thick legs buckled, the hands broke at the wrists, the head came forward with a limp jerk, and the man who had been known over the South Pacific as a pirate tripped forward and sprawled in death.

Smoke released the trigger and relaxed slowly. His words were low as he said, "Well, you asked for it."

The thick legs buckled, the hands broke at the wrists, the head came forward with a limp jerk, and the man who had been known over the South Pacific as a pirate tripped forward and sprawled in death.

CHAPTER FIVE

TWO weary ships came back to the island's harbor, shrouded in the lurid softness of the tropical night, to drop anchors side by side in the quietness of the lagoon, as though they were now as companionable as they had been hateful before.

In the cabin of the *Witch,* Smoke was taking care of the last wounded man aboard the ships—himself. Beneath the soft yellow light which spread out from the gimbaled hurricane lantern above him, he carefully adjusted bandages over his battered shoulders and patted adhesive tape into place with a gesture that was both weary and triumphant.

A smile crept across his tired face as he heard the purr of a motorboat coming toward the ships from the slip below the house of Chan Tso-lan and he glanced at the charting table where a white wooden box sat in all serenity.

The swish of felt slippers approached the passageway leading to Smoke's cabin, to stop at the doorway and be replaced by a smooth, controlled voice.

"Good evening, Mr. Engel," said Chan, his eyes flickering over the room and finally coming to rest upon the white box. "I see that your mission has been successful."

"Yeah," agreed Smoke. "Almost. All I want now, Chan, is the cash in hand and the loan papers on the *Witch.*"

Chan stepped into the circle of light and the beams reflected upon the greasy, hairless skull. The Chinaman's robes fell about him and swirled voluminously upon the planking, giving the impression of enormous size to the fat bulk they enclosed.

Chan drew forth a sheaf of papers and a packet of green slips which were surmounted by a hundred-dollar bill. The bank wrapping of this last gave to understand that the packet was worth ten thousand dollars.

Smoke glanced at the papers, saw seemingly unlimited typewriting, then took the bills.

He glanced at the marking and at the green sides of the packet and then nodded his head toward the white box.

With the swiftness of an uncoiling snake, Chan reached out and snatched up his pearls to thrust the box into the sash about his waist. Then he whirled to the door and vanished, leaving the sound of hurried steps in his wake.

Smoke looked at the packets he held in his hand and then smiled toward the fresh sound of the starting motor. But his smile was short-lived. His lips shot into a straight, hard line as he eyed the papers.

"Phony!" he bellowed. "The dirty yellow rat!" Quickly he stripped off the wrappings from the bills and found that the entire sheaf contained but one hundred dollars surmounting green paper. And there were no signatures on the loan papers.

All tiredness vanished from him as he sprang to the door and thundered across the deck to the rail, staring out into the blackness toward the sound of a sputtering motor. A cry from his tense lips brought a bandaged Chamorro sailor to his side with a flashlight and rifle, and Smoke grasped the items with a savage wrench.

The powerful beams of the five-cell torch shot out whitely across the black lagoon, hovered over the water, and then stabbed straight into the grinning face of Chan as he gave the *Witch* a triumphant look.

Though the retreating boat was over two hundred yards away, the sound of Chan's voice purred clearly back to Smoke.

"He who laughs!" jeered Chan. And then the words slid off into a crackle of Chinese.

Smoke was slow in turning off the light, for his bandaged hands rendered his fingers clumsy. He threw himself flat down in the scupper and dragged the startled brown sailor with him. Rifle bullets smashed into the timber and whined viciously out into the blackness.

Somewhere in all the darkness Chan had riflemen stationed to cover his swift retreat, and the beam of the light had given the key to Smoke's whereabouts.

Outrigger canoes were bobbing on the quiet water ready to smash hot death into the *Witch* should any attempt be made to pursue Chan. The strategy of the move was apparent, for even the bravest of men would think twice before following Chan into his house ashore.

But Smoke gave little thought to the riflemen as he plunged aft toward the longboat which hung in the davits. Two Chamorros lowered away on the blocks and then slid down to the launched craft to pick up ready oars and look to Smoke for orders.

The motorboat was still purring and, though far away,

Smoke knew that he had a very good chance of catching up with the man who had played him traitor. For the boat used by Chan did well to log off four knots while the longboat could lunge ahead at six.

Tense against the tiller, Smoke barked his stroke orders and the dim hulk of the *Witch* fell rapidly away. Phosphorous gleamed in pools where the oars bit into the water, twice on either side of the craft, each time the straining brown backs gave the sweeps a lusty pull.

Smoke counted them in rhythm and tried to pick out his direction without giving his exact location. He knew that Chan's men were listening to the creak of oarlocks and he knew that one streak of light would garner a leaden hurricane from the waiting rifles.

Far ahead Smoke saw the white stern of the motorboat growing more distinct with each passing minute. Chan, too, heard the pursuit and was not long in attempting to avoid apprehension.

A flashlight beam streaked and darted about the lagoon until it finally came to rest squarely upon the body of Smoke, who stood upright, dressed in telltale whites, in the stern.

The instant the light hit him, Smoke heard the joyous bark of hungry rifles as the men squeezed down upon a perfect target.

The only sign Smoke gave that he understood and heard the whining snaps about him, was to increase the stroke tempo. The longboat was now within a few feet of Chan and the bullets ceased as Chinamen laid down their guns to take up paddles.

Close beside the motorboat, Smoke could see five men on the other's thwarts. He jerked out the pistol at his side and, holding the weapon aloft, jumped the remaining distance of a yard to land solidly in the motorboat.

A Chinese raised a rifle and shot. But before the yellow finger could release the trigger, Smoke hammered the man down with lead and saw the body topple back into the dark water, where it would soon be torn to bits by barracudas.

Arms and hands sought to pull the white man down, sought to push him over the side, sought to batter him with oars and gun stocks.

Cries from across the water told Smoke that reinforcements would soon arrive for Chan, and he knew that he must work fast if he wished to live out the night.

The two Chamorros were now in the fight and their war cries were shrill and awful in the darkness. The motorboat lurched drunkenly, spilling water over the gunwales as the impact of blows and bodies smashed against the frail sides.

Chan, in the stern, crowded back as far as possible, hugging the white box in his sash, seeing the fight as a dark blur before him. His right hand brought out a pistol which he leveled at the bodies before him in the hope that he would be able to distinguish Smoke.

Smoke smashed a Chinaman in the face and knocked him over the side into the water which was already beginning to boil with expectant and feasting sea beasts. As he drew back his fist, the white man felt himself struck in the middle and hit athwart at his legs which unbalanced him, making him stumble back perilously close to the gunwale.

One of the Chamorros was struck down to the bottom of the boat and as Smoke passed over him, the brown sailor reached up with a feeble hand and caught hold of Smoke's ankle to save him from plunging down to instant death in the water.

Smoke came back to the remaining three men with fists which hammered a tattoo of destruction. He sent one of his assailants reeling back toward Chan in the stern and was quick to follow up his advantage against the remaining two.

Of his second Chamorro seaman, Smoke could see or hear nothing and he surmised that the man was either knocked out in the boat or was being torn to bits by the savage fish in the water.

Jumping over a thwart, the white man lunged aft where he knew Chan must be, only to be struck from behind by a glancing blow from a rifle butt. He staggered back, threw out an arm, and found that he had caught hold of one of the men.

The scream which split the air was one of sheer terror, for Smoke swung the Oriental clear from the planks and held him aloft, to send him aft as a human projectile.

The crash of the body was followed by another scream—that of Chan—and Smoke stopped to try to see the swindler.

That moment of inaction was fatal. Men from the outrigger canoes were now arriving and their medley of howls rose to the stars as they scrambled out of their small boats into the craft.

The hard press of bodies bore Smoke down to the bottom of the motorboat and though he struck out with all the strength at his command, his blows seemed to have no effect upon his immediate circumstance.

He heard splashes and knew that he was knocking Chan's men into the lagoon, but he knew that two would spring upon him for every one he knocked away.

At last strong hands held him fast and motionless in the bottom, and though he cursed and tried to move, Smoke was sure that his last day on earth had arrived.

CHAPTER SIX

CHAN lighted his electric torch and played the beam before him, letting it come to rest squarely on Smoke's face. Though the white man could see nothing of the swindler's countenance, he knew the expression which must be there. It required no imagination to visualize the savage glare of triumph which overrode the features.

A pistol jutted out from behind the torch and the light played evilly upon the glinting blue barrel. A yellow finger tensed on the trigger as the muzzle pointed straight between Smoke's eyes.

"Now," purred Chan, "before I send you to your doubtful reward, permit me to properly thank you for your favors. You have given me back the black pearls, worth half a million dollars; you have presented me with the *Witch,* which I have always wanted; and in addition to this, my friend, you have given me the *Negrito,* which I can most certainly use.

"And now, with your permission, Mr. Engel, I take your life as swiftly as possible." Chan laughed harshly and the yellow finger came slowly back.

Smoke stared at the muzzle with a hypnotic fascination, knowing that he would never see the face which would send a hot metal slug boring into his brain. And until that moment Smoke had never realized how terribly much he wanted to live.

Chan suddenly screamed with terror and Smoke looked up beyond the gun to see the felt slippers cant up into the beam. The gun pointed up and flamed, sending the shot intended for Smoke straight into the heavens.

Scream after scream held the entire group in the boat motionless with horror. The felt slippers slid back and the light crashed into the boat to reverse its beam and point straight up into the writhing body of Chan.

Slowly the hulk of yellow flesh slid back over the stern, and then, with one last cry which ended in a sob, splashed into the water to be dragged far down into the black depths. Only a swirl of phosphorescent water marked the grave of Chan Tso-lan.

The men about Smoke were suddenly released from the awful terror which had held them and they now jumped aft to look down, completely forgetting Smoke. With a lunge back, Smoke snatched up a rifle which lay forgotten beneath the thwarts and slammed a cartridge into the chamber.

But there was now no fight in the followers of Chan. Without a leader they were as docile as sheep, and after a brief moment's hesitation, Smoke commanded them to return to their outrigger canoes and push off for shore.

When the men had gone, Smoke stepped back to the stern and looked at the spot where Chan had disappeared, to see the answer to the Oriental's death.

A barracuda, its teeth glistening in the light of the torch Smoke held, came to the surface for a brief instant and then shot back into the bloody water. Smoke realized then what had happened.

One of Chan's robes had dangled into the water, giving the sea beast a target at which to strike. And when the barracuda had hit the robe, its teeth had become imbedded in the cloth and by trying to get away it had pulled down Chan. Upon him it was now feasting.

Smoke shuddered and started to turn away, the thought in his mind that all he had gained by the encounter was the *Negrito* and the ownership of the *Witch* once more. But then, Chan had promised ten thousand dollars, and—

The beam licked greenly down into the waves and caught a glimmer of white floating on the water. It was only idle curiosity which made Smoke turn and look more closely at the splotch.

With an oar he reached out and brought the object closer in toward the motorboat, to finally realize that it was what he had guessed it to be.

In his hand he held the wooden box which contained a half-million dollars in black pearls!

Smoke smiled slowly and then looked back at the water as the irony of fate came home to him. By playing traitor, Chan had not only lost his pearls to the white trader, but had also lost his life.

The two Chamorros shook their battered heads and grinned as they rowed Smoke back to the waiting *Witch*.

STORY PREVIEW

NOW that you've just ventured through some of the captivating tales in the Stories from the Golden Age collection by L. Ron Hubbard, turn the page and enjoy a preview of *The Trail of the Red Diamonds*. Join Lieutenant Jonathan Daly on a fateful expedition into the depths of China to unearth a fabulous fortune in red diamonds, leading him down a dark maze of betrayal, espionage and death—with more on the line than he ever expected.

THE TRAIL OF THE RED DIAMONDS

I first ran across the trail in a hospital, two months after leaving the Gran Chaco behind me. As souvenirs of that continual war I had collected two bullet holes and a case of malaria, and I was certainly in no condition to go racing off to China the way I did.

The doctors told me so and my friends threw up their hands in horror, but that didn't deter me. The urge was too strong. I felt that if I didn't go, I'd be eaten up by the gnawing determination to find the red diamonds of Kublai Khan.

I had come across an original manuscript of Marco Polo's. The man that lent it to me did not know its value. And even when I told him, he laughed at me. I had plenty of money and I didn't need his help, but even so, I had him lined up for a cut in the event of success.

Most copies of Marco Polo's *Travels* leave out a great deal. They have to because it is difficult to decipher, and even more difficult to translate. But, for my own amusement, I had been working on it for almost a month, while laid up.

Halfway through the volume I read a paragraph about a chest of fabulous red stones which glittered "like the sun through red-stained quartz." Stones which would cut even metal. At first I thought he meant rubies. Then, on further description, I understood that he could mean diamonds and only diamonds. Red diamonds.

The things were worth millions! Many millions!

My appetite for the unusual was whetted by that paragraph. I made a note of it for later reference, and it was a good thing that I did. Otherwise I might never have connected it with another, later, item.

Further on in the book, the famous traveler stated that the beliefs of the Asiatics were scarcely understandable to Western minds. He stated further that his host, the emperor of Asia, Kublai Khan, had requested that a chest of glittering red stones be buried with him to light his way to heaven and to serve as offerings to the gods.

Marco Polo, in his painstaking way, had covered years in the writing of his book. The two remarks were far apart in inscription—months, perhaps.

Suddenly I saw the light. I sat up straight in bed, gripping the tattered pages in both hands, shivering with excitement. I was wholly unconscious of my weakened condition, wholly forgetful of the Chaco. I saw only one thing. A chest of red diamonds buried in the grave of Kublai Khan!

I threw the covers back and yelled for my clothes. If Kublai Khan's grave were still intact, it meant that a fortune in rare stones had lain untouched for centuries! And I meant to be the first man there, whether I was sick or well.

An hour later I was in a telegraph station writing a cable to Jim Lange in China. I used a code book that five of us carried. Jim Lange and the other three had been with me in

South America, and we had promised when we separated that when anything good turned up, we would let the one nearest to the scene know. As luck would have it, Jim Lange was in Peking.

I had no qualms about setting the whole thing down baldly. No one else would ever know what I wrote. Besides, the code was so condensed that the entire message, including the address, only took eight words.

I told Jim to get a caravan of camels together and to assemble a company of soldiers, and I knew that he would.

Bolstered by excitement, I flew across the continent and sailed from Seattle. Eighteen days later, I was in Kobe, Japan, negotiating a passage on a tub of rust across the Yellow Sea. Five days after that, I was in the Gulf of Campechi, watching the squat concrete forts loom up on the horizon. That evening, I stood outside the railway station at Taku, awaiting the doubtful arrival of a train to Peking, China.

A cold bitter wind was sweeping down from the Gobi, hundreds of miles to the north. Curls of yellow dust swooped around the station's brick corners. Beggars tugged at the skirt of my trench coat, whining for pennies. Soldiers lounged against their baggage, stoically waiting for the train.

I asked the station agent, a wizened Chinese, when the train would come.

"Right away," he said glibly. "Maybe tomorrow morning. Maybe next month. Bandits bad near Tientsin." That was all I could get out of him.

If you've ever been in that hole they call Taku, you'll understand what I was up against. I was racked with excitement.

In spite of the wind, I was sweating. And in spite of the sweat, I felt that someone was pouring ice water down my spine. Malaria leaves you that way.

There were no hotels. The station was so filthy that a man couldn't find a place to lie down, but even so, at midnight, I was so tired that I was almost ready to flop in the middle of the platform, coolies and beggars notwithstanding.

It was then that the young Chinese officer in the gray overcoat approached me. It was dark and I couldn't see his face. But by the light from the station window he could see that I was an American.

He asked me if I wanted to go to a hotel. He said that he had just received word from upcountry that the train would not be there until late the next afternoon. He looked at me more closely.

"Whassa matter? You blong sick?"

"I'm all right," I said. "Where's your hotel?"

I let him lead me across the tracks toward a cluster of lights which appeared to be the main part of the ten-house town. When we were a hundred yards away from the station, I could see him only by the green light of a switch.

Then he whirled on me. His stature seemed to double. His hand darted out and caught at my trench coat. I should have been prepared for that, but I was not. Weak and cold and tired, it took me an instant to collect my wits. And that instant was enough for him. His right hand snapped toward my shirt pockets. Something thin and flat and square came away with a rending of cloth.

His left fist smashed me in the mouth, and I staggered back, trying to keep my balance, tripping over the ties. The whole thing took place in a split second. Then he was running, a vague, flitting shadow in the night.

GLOSSARY

STORIES FROM THE GOLDEN AGE *reflect the words and expressions used in the 1930s and 1940s, adding unique flavor and authenticity to the tales. While a character's speech may often reflect regional origins, it also can convey attitudes common in the day. So that readers can better grasp such cultural and historical terms, uncommon words or expressions of the era, the following glossary has been provided.*

Aloadin or **Hasan ibn Sabbah:** leader of an Islamic religious cult called the *Ismalilis* and later the *Assassins,* derived from the Arabic word meaning "smokers of hashish." The Assassins resided in a pirate state and terrorized western Asia in the twelfth and thirteenth centuries by attacking the heads of government and religious leaders. Aloadin exerted a strong power over his followers. He created special gardens where actual milk and honey flowed and where beautiful damsels skilled in dancing and music sported in the gardens and palaces. Through the use of hashish, he cast the young men into a deep sleep, whereupon they awoke in "paradise." After spending a few days in the gardens they were promised to be returned there, dead or alive, in exchange for certain deeds. Thus assassinations were ordered and dedicatedly executed by these young men without regard for their personal lives.

bagaturs: (Mongolian) warriors, military commanders or epic heroes.

belaying pin: a large wooden or metal pin that fits into a hole in a rail on a ship or boat, and to which a rope can be fastened.

bitt: a vertical post, usually one of a pair, set on the deck of a ship and used for securing cables, lines for towing, etc.

black sand: a heavy, glossy, partly magnetic mixture of fine sands. Black sand is an indicator of the presence of gold or other precious metals.

bowsprit: a spar projecting from the upper end of the bow of a sailing vessel, for holding and supporting a sail.

bull fiddle: also called a bass fiddle; the largest and lowest member of the violin family.

bulwarks: solid walls enclosing the perimeters of a weather or main deck for the protection of persons or objects on deck.

Chamorro: a people inhabiting the Mariana Islands; also the language of these people.

copra: the dried kernel or meat of the coconut from which coconut oil is obtained.

Coral Sea: southwest arm of the Pacific Ocean, extending from the western Australian coast more than 1,400 miles (2,253 km) east to the New Hebrides Islands and to New Guinea and the Solomon Islands in the north. The Great Barrier Reef lies along its western edge.

Cossacks: members of a people of southern European Russia and adjacent parts of Asia, noted as cavalrymen especially during tzarist times. The Cossacks, known for their horses and horsemanship, were considered to be unequaled anywhere on Earth. In 1892, a troupe of Cossack daredevil riders joined the Buffalo Bill's Wild West show, traveling to London and then to America in 1893. Intrigued by the Cossacks' trick riding and stunts on their galloping horses, the Western cowboys soon introduced variations to American rodeo.

crosstree: the raised wooden pieces at the front and rear of the saddle that form a high pommel or horn in the front and cantle in the back.

Dante: Dante Alighieri (1265–1321), Italian poet best known for his work *The Divine Comedy,* which is the story of a journey through Hell, Purgatory and Paradise. The journey through Hell is often referred to independently as "Dante's *Inferno.*"

davits: any of various cranelike devices, used singly or in pairs, for supporting, raising and lowering boats, anchors and cargo over a hatchway or side of a ship.

double eagle: a gold coin of the US with a denomination of twenty dollars, produced from 1850 to 1933. Prior to 1850, eagles with a denomination of ten dollars were the largest denomination of US coin, and since the twenty-dollar gold piece had twice the value of the eagle, it was designated a "double eagle."

Drake: Sir Francis Drake (1545–1596); British admiral, explorer and privateer. He was the first Englishman to circumnavigate the globe. A naval war hero, his legendary defeat of the Spanish Armada off the southern coast of England in 1588 was the turning point for England's rise to naval power. The Spanish referred to Drake as a pirate and nicknamed him The Dragon.

ducks: slacks or trousers; pants made of a heavy, plain-weave cotton fabric.

dum: a bullet with a soft front that increases in size when it hits its target, causing serious injuries. Also called dum-dum bullets.

forked saddle: a saddle designed with a fork at the front, as on a Western saddle. The fork, which provides the base for the horn, is the piece that holds together the two parallel bars that rest along both sides of the horse's back. Originally, this part of the saddle's structure was made from the fork of a tree, hence its name. It is the structural piece that gives the front of the saddle its characteristic shape.

Genghis Khan: (1162?–1227) Mongol conqueror who founded the largest land empire in history and whose armies, known for their use of terror, conquered many territories and slaughtered the populations of entire cities.

G-men: government men; agents of the Federal Bureau of Investigation.

Gobi: Asia's largest desert, located in China and southern Mongolia.

Golden Mountains: also known as the Altay Mountains; *Altay* means *Mountains of Gold* in Mongolian. The mountains are located in Central Asia where Russia, China and Mongolia come together.

Gran Chaco: region in south central South America, covering about 250,000 square miles (647,500 sq km), and encompassing part of Argentina, Paraguay and Bolivia. It is the location of the Chaco War (1932–1935), a border dispute fought between Bolivia and Paraguay over control of a great part of this region of South America that was incorrectly thought to be rich in oil.

grappling hooks: composite hooks attached to ropes designed to be thrown or projected a distance so that the hooks will engage with the target.

gunwale: the upper edge of the side of a boat. Originally a gunwale was a platform where guns were mounted, and was designed to accommodate the additional stresses imposed by the artillery being used.

halyards: ropes used for raising and lowering sails.

Headless Horseman: from the short story written in 1812 by Washington Irving called "The Legend of Sleepy Hollow." Schoolmaster Ichabod Crane of the town of Sleepy Hollow, dismissing the legend of the Headless Horseman, later flees in terror from the Horseman and is chased over a bridge never to be seen again. The Headless Horseman, an undead ghostly character, was said to have lost his head to a cannon ball during an unnamed battle.

Hotel du Pekin: in the 1930s it was considered one of the finest hotels in the Orient. Built in 1917, the hotel had 200 rooms with baths, a tea hall with nightly dancing and its own orchestra for classical dinner music. It also had a spacious roof garden overlooking the Forbidden City and the Legation Quarter (walled city within the city exclusively for foreigners).

houris: in Muslim belief, any of the dark-eyed virgins of perfect beauty believed to live with the blessed in Paradise.

Kalgan: a city in northeast China near the Great Wall that served as both a commercial and a military center. Kalgan means "gate in a barrier" or "frontier" in Mongolian. It is the eastern entry into China from Inner Mongolia.

Khans: family of Mongol conquerors, beginning with Genghis Khan (1162?–1227), who founded the largest land empire in history and whose armies, known for their use of terror, conquered many territories and slaughtered the populations of entire cities. The Khan reign ended with Kublai Khan (1215–1294), military leader and grandson of Genghis Khan.

knot: a unit of speed, equal to one nautical mile, or about 1.15 miles, per hour.

Kobe: a seaport in southern Japan.

Kublai Khan: (1215–1294) military leader, grandson of Genghis Khan and the last ruler of the Khan empire.

longboat: the longest boat carried by a sailing ship.

Luray Cavern: a large underground cavern in Luray, Virginia, discovered in 1878.

Mammoth Cave: longest system of caves in the world with more than 365 miles (587 km) explored. It is located in south central Kentucky.

Mannlicher: a type of rifle equipped with a manually operated sliding bolt for loading cartridges for firing, as opposed to the more common rotating bolt of other rifles. Mannlicher rifles were considered reasonably strong and accurate.

Marco Polo: (1254?–1324?) Italian traveler who explored Asia (1271–1295). His book, *The Travels of Marco Polo,* was the only account of the Far East available to Europeans until the seventeenth century.

Mayas: a member of a group of Indian peoples, chiefly of Yucatán, Belize and Guatemala, whose languages are Mayan.

Melanesians: people native to a division of Oceania in the southwest Pacific Ocean, comprising the islands northeast of Australia and south of the equator. It includes the Solomon Islands. The Melanesian people primarily fish and farm, and supplement their economy by exporting cacao, copra (coconut) and copper.

Morgan: Sir Henry Morgan (1635?–1688), a Welsh buccaneer in the Americas. His brutal hostilities against the Spanish colonies in the Caribbean are known for their skillful execution, at times, against great odds. An exaggerated account of his exploits, written by one of his crew, created his popular reputation as a bloodthirsty pirate.

Nubians: natives or inhabitants of an area of southern Egypt and northern Sudan corresponding to the ancient region of Nubia.

oxide ore: mineralized rock in which some of the original minerals have been oxidized. Oxidation tends to make the ore more porous; that facilitates the flow of solutions into the rock. This effect is particularly important for oxidized gold ore, as it permits more complete permeation of cyanide solutions so that minute particles of gold in the interior of the mineral grains can be readily dissolved.

panner: a container in which gold, or other heavy and valuable metal, is separated from gravel or other substances by agitation.

Peking: now Beijing, China.

poop deck: a deck that constitutes the roof of a cabin built in the aft part of the ship. The name originates from the Latin *puppis*, for the elevated stern deck.

quarterdeck: the rear part of the upper deck of a ship, usually reserved for officers.

quirt: a riding whip with a short handle and a braided leather lash.

rovers: pirates.

rudder: a means of steering a boat or ship, usually in the form of a pivoting blade under the water, mounted at the stern and controlled by a wheel or handle.

rudder chains: loose chains or ropes that fasten the rudder to the ship to prevent its loss in case it gets out of position, and for operating it in case the wheel is broken.

Scheherazade: the female narrator of *The Arabian Nights*, who during one thousand and one adventurous nights saved her life by entertaining her husband, the king, with stories.

schooner: a fast sailing ship with at least two masts and with sails set lengthwise.

scuppers: gutters along the edge of the deck that drain into openings in the side of a ship that allow water to run off.

Shamo desert: Chinese name for the Gobi Desert; Asia's largest desert located in China and southern Mongolia.

single jack: working with a single jack, a short-handled hammer with a three- to four-pound head, used for punching holes in rock.

Snider: a rifle formerly used in the British service. It was invented by American Jacob Snider in the mid-1800s.

The Snider was a breech-loading rifle, derived from its muzzle-loading predecessor called the Enfield.

Solomon Islands: a group of islands northeast of Australia. They form a double chain of six large islands, about twenty medium-sized ones and numerous smaller islets and reefs.

sourdoughs: settlers or prospectors, especially in the western United States or northwest Canada and Alaska.

spent bullet: a bullet shot from a firearm that reaches an object without having sufficient force to penetrate or pass through it. Even if not fatal, a spent bullet can still cause serious injury.

Springfield: any of several types of rifle, named after Springfield, Massachusetts, the site of a federal armory that made the rifles.

Sunken Road at Waterloo: a sunken road that ran along a ridge and formed the allied lines in the Battle of Waterloo (1815). The sunken road hindered Napoleon's attack on the British and allies, as the horsemen fell into the road that was invisible until they were upon it.

sweeps: long, heavy oars.

Taku: site of forts built in the 1500s to defend Tientsin against foreign invasion. The forts are located by the Hai River, 37 miles (60 km) southeast of Tientsin.

Tartar: a member of any of the various tribes, chiefly Mongolian and Turkish, who, originally under the leadership of Genghis Khan, overran Asia and much of eastern Europe in the Middle Ages. Also a member of the descendants of these people.

thwart: a seat across a boat, especially one used by a rower.

Tientsin: seaport located southeast of Peking; China's third largest city and major transportation and trading center. Tientsin was a "Treaty Port," a generic term used to denote Chinese cities open to foreign residence and trade, usually the result of a treaty.

Timur the Limper: (1336–1405) a name for Timur Lenk or Tamerlane meaning "Timur the Lame." Timur was a Mongol conqueror and the name is supposed to have reflected the battle wounds he received.

Yellow Sea: an arm of the Pacific Ocean between the Chinese mainland and the Korean Peninsula. It connects with the East China Sea to the south.

Yucatán: a peninsula mostly in southeastern Mexico between the Caribbean Sea and the Gulf of Mexico.

L. Ron Hubbard in the Golden Age of Pulp Fiction

In writing an adventure story
a writer has to know that he is adventuring
for a lot of people who cannot.
The writer has to take them here and there
about the globe and show them
excitement and love and realism.
As long as that writer is living the part of an
adventurer when he is hammering
the keys, he is succeeding with his story.

Adventuring is a state of mind.
If you adventure through life, you have a
good chance to be a success on paper.

Adventure doesn't mean globe-trotting,
exactly, and it doesn't mean great deeds.
Adventuring is like art.
You have to live it to make it real.

—L. Ron Hubbard

L. Ron Hubbard and American Pulp Fiction

BORN March 13, 1911, L. Ron Hubbard lived a life at least as expansive as the stories with which he enthralled a hundred million readers through a fifty-year career.

Originally hailing from Tilden, Nebraska, he spent his formative years in a classically rugged Montana, replete with the cowpunchers, lawmen and desperadoes who would later people his Wild West adventures. And lest anyone imagine those adventures were drawn from vicarious experience, he was not only breaking broncs at a tender age, he was also among the few whites ever admitted into Blackfoot society as a bona fide blood brother. While if only to round out an otherwise rough and tumble youth, his mother was that rarity of her time—a thoroughly educated woman—who introduced her son to the classics of Occidental literature even before his seventh birthday.

But as any dedicated L. Ron Hubbard reader will attest, his world extended far beyond Montana. In point of fact, and as the son of a United States naval officer, by the age of eighteen he had traveled over a quarter of a million miles. Included therein were three Pacific crossings to a then still mysterious Asia, where he ran with the likes of Her British Majesty's agent-in-place

L. Ron Hubbard, left, at Congressional Airport, Washington, DC, 1931, with members of George Washington University flying club.

for North China, and the last in the line of Royal Magicians from the court of Kublai Khan. For the record, L. Ron Hubbard was also among the first Westerners to gain admittance to forbidden Tibetan monasteries below Manchuria, and his photographs of China's Great Wall long graced American geography texts.

Upon his return to the United States and a hasty completion of his interrupted high school education, the young Ron Hubbard entered George Washington University. There, as fans of his aerial adventures may have heard, he earned his wings as a pioneering barnstormer at the dawn of American aviation. He also earned a place in free-flight record books for the longest sustained flight above Chicago. Moreover, as a roving reporter for *Sportsman Pilot* (featuring his first professionally penned articles), he further helped inspire a generation of pilots who would take America to world airpower.

Immediately beyond his sophomore year, Ron embarked on the first of his famed ethnological expeditions, initially to then untrammeled Caribbean shores (descriptions of which would later fill a whole series of West Indies mystery-thrillers). That the Puerto Rican interior would also figure into the future of Ron Hubbard stories was likewise no accident. For in addition to cultural studies of the island, a 1932–33

LRH expedition is rightly remembered as conducting the first complete mineralogical survey of a Puerto Rico under United States jurisdiction.

There was many another adventure along this vein: As a lifetime member of the famed Explorers Club, L. Ron Hubbard charted North Pacific waters with the first shipboard radio direction finder, and so pioneered a long-range navigation system universally employed until the late twentieth century. While not to put too fine an edge on it, he also held a rare Master Mariner's license to pilot any vessel, of any tonnage in any ocean.

Yet lest we stray too far afield, there is an LRH note at this juncture in his saga, and it reads in part:

"I started out writing for the pulps, writing the best I knew, writing for every mag on the stands, slanting as well as I could."

To which one might add: His earliest submissions date from the summer of 1934, and included tales drawn from true-to-life Asian adventures, with characters roughly modeled on British/American intelligence operatives he had known in Shanghai. His early Westerns were similarly peppered with details drawn from personal experience. Although therein lay a first hard lesson from the often cruel world of the pulps. His first Westerns were soundly rejected as lacking the authenticity of a Max Brand yarn

Capt. L. Ron Hubbard in Ketchikan, Alaska, 1940, on his Alaskan Radio Experimental Expedition, the first of three voyages conducted under the Explorers Club flag.

(a particularly frustrating comment given L. Ron Hubbard's Westerns came straight from his Montana homeland, while Max Brand was a mediocre New York poet named Frederick Schiller Faust, who turned out implausible six-shooter tales from the terrace of an Italian villa).

Nevertheless, and needless to say, L. Ron Hubbard persevered and soon earned a reputation as among the most publishable names in pulp fiction, with a ninety percent placement rate of first-draft manuscripts. He was also among the most prolific, averaging between seventy and a hundred thousand words a month. Hence the rumors that L. Ron Hubbard had redesigned a typewriter for faster keyboard action and pounded out manuscripts on a continuous roll of butcher paper to save the precious seconds it took to insert a single sheet of paper into manual typewriters of the day.

That all L. Ron Hubbard stories did not run beneath said byline is yet another aspect of pulp fiction lore. That is, as publishers periodically rejected manuscripts from top-drawer authors if only to avoid paying top dollar, L. Ron Hubbard and company just as frequently replied with submissions under various pseudonyms. In Ron's case, the

A Man of Many Names

Between 1934 and 1950, L. Ron Hubbard authored more than fifteen million words of fiction in more than two hundred classic publications. To supply his fans and editors with stories across an array of genres and pulp titles, he adopted fifteen pseudonyms in addition to his already renowned L. Ron Hubbard byline.

Winchester Remington Colt
Lt. Jonathan Daly
Capt. Charles Gordon
Capt. L. Ron Hubbard
Bernard Hubbel
Michael Keith
Rene Lafayette
Legionnaire 148
Legionnaire 14830
Ken Martin
Scott Morgan
Lt. Scott Morgan
Kurt von Rachen
Barry Randolph
Capt. Humbert Reynolds

L. Ron Hubbard, circa 1930, at the outset of a literary career that would finally span half a century.

list included: Rene Lafayette, Captain Charles Gordon, Lt. Scott Morgan and the notorious Kurt von Rachen—supposedly on the lam for a murder rap, while hammering out two-fisted prose in Argentina. The point: While L. Ron Hubbard as Ken Martin spun stories of Southeast Asian intrigue, LRH as Barry Randolph authored tales of romance on the Western range—which, stretching between a dozen genres is how he came to stand among the two hundred elite authors providing close to a million tales through the glory days of American Pulp Fiction.

In evidence of exactly that, by 1936 L. Ron Hubbard was literally leading pulp fiction's elite as president of New York's American Fiction Guild. Members included a veritable pulp hall of fame: Lester "Doc Savage" Dent, Walter "The Shadow" Gibson, and the legendary Dashiell Hammett—to cite but a few.

Also in evidence of just where L. Ron Hubbard stood within his first two years on the American pulp circuit: By the spring of 1937, he was ensconced in Hollywood, adopting a Caribbean thriller for Columbia Pictures, remembered today as *The Secret of Treasure Island.* Comprising fifteen thirty-minute episodes, the L. Ron Hubbard screenplay led to the most profitable matinée serial in Hollywood history. In accord with Hollywood culture, he was thereafter continually called upon

The 1937 Secret of Treasure Island, *a fifteen-episode serial adapted for the screen by L. Ron Hubbard from his novel,* Murder at Pirate Castle.

to rewrite/doctor scripts—most famously for long-time friend and fellow adventurer Clark Gable.

In the interim—and herein lies another distinctive chapter of the L. Ron Hubbard story—he continually worked to open Pulp Kingdom gates to up-and-coming authors. Or, for that matter, anyone who wished to write. It was a fairly unconventional stance, as markets were already thin and competition razor sharp. But the fact remains, it was an L. Ron Hubbard hallmark that he vehemently lobbied on behalf of young authors—regularly supplying instructional articles to trade journals, guest-lecturing to short story classes at George Washington University and Harvard, and even founding his own creative writing competition. It was established in 1940, dubbed the Golden Pen, and guaranteed winners both New York representation and publication in *Argosy.*

But it was John W. Campbell Jr.'s *Astounding Science Fiction* that finally proved the most memorable LRH vehicle. While every fan of L. Ron Hubbard's galactic epics undoubtedly knows the story, it nonetheless bears repeating: By late 1938, the pulp publishing magnate of Street & Smith was determined to revamp *Astounding Science Fiction* for broader readership. In particular, senior editorial director F. Orlin Tremaine called for stories with a stronger *human element.* When acting editor John W. Campbell balked, preferring his spaceship-driven tales, Tremaine enlisted Hubbard. Hubbard, in turn, replied with the genre's first truly *character-driven* works, wherein heroes are pitted not against bug-eyed monsters but the mystery and majesty of deep space itself—and thus was launched the Golden Age of Science Fiction.

The names alone are enough to quicken the pulse of any science fiction aficionado, including LRH friend and protégé, Robert Heinlein, Isaac Asimov, A. E. van Vogt and Ray Bradbury. Moreover, when coupled with LRH stories of fantasy, we further come to what's rightly been described as the foundation of every modern tale of horror: L. Ron Hubbard's immortal *Fear*. It was rightly proclaimed by Stephen King as one of the very few works to genuinely warrant that overworked term "classic"—as in: *"This is a classic tale of creeping, surreal menace and horror. . . . This is one of the really, really good ones."*

L. Ron Hubbard, 1948, among fellow science fiction luminaries at the World Science Fiction Convention in Toronto.

To accommodate the greater body of L. Ron Hubbard fantasies, Street & Smith inaugurated *Unknown*—a classic pulp if there ever was one, and wherein readers were soon thrilling to the likes of *Typewriter in the Sky* and *Slaves of Sleep* of which Frederik Pohl would declare: *"There are bits and pieces from Ron's work that became part of the language in ways that very few other writers managed."*

And, indeed, at J. W. Campbell Jr.'s insistence, Ron was regularly drawing on themes from the Arabian Nights and so introducing readers to a world of genies, jinn, Aladdin and Sinbad—all of which, of course, continue to float through cultural mythology to this day.

At least as influential in terms of post-apocalypse stories was L. Ron Hubbard's 1940 *Final Blackout*. Generally acclaimed as the finest anti-war novel of the decade and among the ten best works of the genre ever authored—here, too, was a tale that would live on in ways few other writers imagined. Hence, the later Robert Heinlein verdict: "Final Blackout *is as perfect a piece of science fiction as has ever been written.*"

Portland, Oregon, 1943; L. Ron Hubbard, captain of the US Navy subchaser PC 815.

Like many another who both lived and wrote American pulp adventure, the war proved a tragic end to Ron's sojourn in the pulps. He served with distinction in four theaters and was highly decorated for commanding corvettes in the North Pacific. He was also grievously wounded in combat, lost many a close friend and colleague and thus resolved to say farewell to pulp fiction and devote himself to what it had supported these many years—namely, his serious research.

But in no way was the LRH literary saga at an end, for as he wrote some thirty years later, in 1980:

"Recently there came a period when I had little to do. This was novel in a life so crammed with busy years, and I decided to amuse myself by writing a novel that was pure *science fiction."*

That work was *Battlefield Earth: A Saga of the Year 3000*. It was an immediate *New York Times* bestseller and, in fact, the first international science fiction blockbuster in decades. It was not, however, L. Ron Hubbard's magnum opus, as that distinction is generally reserved for his next and final work: The 1.2 million word *Mission Earth*.

Final Blackout *is as perfect a piece of science fiction as has ever been written.*

—Robert Heinlein

How he managed those 1.2 million words in just over twelve months is yet another piece of the L. Ron Hubbard legend. But the fact remains, he did indeed author a ten-volume *dekalogy* that lives in publishing history for the fact that each and every volume of the series was also a *New York Times* bestseller.

Moreover, as subsequent generations discovered L. Ron Hubbard through republished works and novelizations of his screenplays, the mere fact of his name on a cover signaled an international bestseller. . . . Until, to date, sales of his works exceed hundreds of millions, and he otherwise remains among the most enduring and widely read authors in literary history. Although as a final word on the tales of L. Ron Hubbard, perhaps it's enough to simply reiterate what editors told readers in the glory days of American Pulp Fiction:

He writes the way he does, brothers, because he's been there, seen it and done it!

THE STORIES FROM THE GOLDEN AGE

Your ticket to adventure starts here with the Stories from the Golden Age collection by master storyteller L. Ron Hubbard. These gripping tales are set in a kaleidoscope of exotic locales and brim with fascinating characters, including some of the most vile villains, dangerous dames and brazen heroes you'll ever get to meet.

The entire collection of over one hundred and fifty stories is being released in a series of eighty books and audiobooks. For an up-to-date listing of available titles, go to www.goldenagestories.com.

AIR ADVENTURE

Arctic Wings
The Battling Pilot
Boomerang Bomber
The Crate Killer
The Dive Bomber
Forbidden Gold
Hurtling Wings
The Lieutenant Takes the Sky
Man-Killers of the Air
On Blazing Wings
Red Death Over China
Sabotage in the Sky
Sky Birds Dare!
The Sky-Crasher
Trouble on His Wings
Wings Over Ethiopia

FAR-FLUNG ADVENTURE

The Adventure of "X"
All Frontiers Are Jealous
The Barbarians
The Black Sultan
Black Towers to Danger
The Bold Dare All
Buckley Plays a Hunch
The Cossack
Destiny's Drum
Escape for Three
Fifty-Fifty O'Brien
The Headhunters
Hell's Legionnaire
He Walked to War
Hostage to Death
Hurricane
The Iron Duke
Machine Gun 21,000
Medals for Mahoney
Price of a Hat
Red Sand
The Sky Devil
The Small Boss of Nunaloha
The Squad That Never Came Back
Starch and Stripes
Tomb of the Ten Thousand Dead
Trick Soldier
While Bugles Blow!
Yukon Madness

SEA ADVENTURE

Cargo of Coffins
The Drowned City
False Cargo
Grounded
Loot of the Shanung
Mister Tidwell, Gunner
The Phantom Patrol
Sea Fangs
Submarine
Twenty Fathoms Down
Under the Black Ensign

TALES FROM THE ORIENT

The Devil—With Wings
The Falcon Killer
Five Mex for a Million
Golden Hell
The Green God
Hurricane's Roar
Inky Odds
Orders Is Orders
Pearl Pirate
The Red Dragon
Spy Killer
Tah
The Trail of the Red Diamonds
Wind-Gone-Mad
Yellow Loot

MYSTERY

The Blow Torch Murder
Brass Keys to Murder
Calling Squad Cars!
The Carnival of Death
The Chee-Chalker
Dead Men Kill
The Death Flyer
Flame City
The Grease Spot
Killer Ape
Killer's Law
The Mad Dog Murder
Mouthpiece
Murder Afloat
The Slickers
They Killed Him Dead

FANTASY

SCIENCE FICTION

WESTERN

The Baron of Coyote River
Blood on His Spurs
Boss of the Lazy B
Branded Outlaw
Cattle King for a Day
Come and Get It
Death Waits at Sundown
Devil's Manhunt
The Ghost Town Gun-Ghost
Gun Boss of Tumbleweed
Gunman!
Gunman's Tally
The Gunner from Gehenna
Hoss Tamer
Johnny, the Town Tamer
King of the Gunmen
The Magic Quirt
Man for Breakfast
The No-Gun Gunhawk
The No-Gun Man
The Ranch That No One Would Buy
Reign of the Gila Monster
Ride 'Em, Cowboy
Ruin at Rio Piedras
Shadows from Boot Hill
Silent Pards
Six-Gun Caballero
Stacked Bullets
Stranger in Town
Tinhorn's Daughter
The Toughest Ranger
Under the Diehard Brand
Vengeance Is Mine!
When Gilhooly Was in Flower